Deadly Combat

Ananda dangled over the middle of the pit; she was held only by a thick hemp rope.

The Old Man turned to Gupta and me. "You two will fight a dozen of Kali's finest," he said.

The thugs appearing in front of the Old Man hardly looked like the best of anything, but they were all big and ugly.

"There's more," I said, beginning to understand the way this devious man's mind worked.

"In this jar are insects, hungry, gnawing, chewing insects. They love the honey smeared on the rope."

It all came to me in a flash. Gupta Dasai and I had to fight our way through a dozen thugs and reach Ananda before the insects gnawed through the rope holding her. If we were killed, she would plunge to her death . . .

NICK CARTER IS IT!

"Nick Carter out-Bonds James Bond."
                    —*Buffalo Evening News*

"Nick Carter is America's #1 espionage agent."
                    —*Variety*

"Nick Carter is razor-sharp suspense."
                    —*King Features*

"Nick Carter is extraordinarily big."
                    —*Bestsellers*

"Nick Carter has attracted an army of addicted readers . . . the books are fast, have plenty of action and just the right degree of sex . . . Nick Carter is the American James Bond, suave, sophisticated, a killer with both the ladies and the enemy."

                    —*The New York Times*

FROM THE NICK CARTER
KILLMASTER SERIES

A Killmaster Spy Chiller

NICK CARTER

THE KALI DEATH CULT

CHARTER BOOKS, NEW YORK

THE KALI DEATH CULT

A Charter Book/published by arrangement with
The Condé Nast Publications, Inc.

PRINTING HISTORY
Charter edition May 1983

ISBN: 0-441-42781-2

Charter Books are published by Charter Communications, Inc.
200 Madison Avenue, New York, New York 10016.
PRINTED IN THE UNITED STATES OF AMERICA

*Dedicated to the men of the
Secret Services of the
United States of America*

ONE

My heart raced as I clutched the hypodermic needle filled with the deadly solution. Back against the cold hospital wall, the tap-tap-tap of footsteps just around the corner, the uncertainty of my target and the chance for discovery made my pulse pound wildly in my temples. Then he came into sight. My training and years of experience took over: my hand steadied, my heart quieted its insane race and I acted.

He never knew what happened.

My forearm circled his throat while my knee drove into the small of his back. Pulled off balance with no hope of recovering, he clawed at my arm. While a natural reaction, it was also the last mistake he ever made. The thin needle laden with succinylcholine chloride plunged into his exposed wrist. He died before he even felt the mild prick at the injection site.

Nick Carter, Killmaster for AXE, had once again performed his mission swiftly, accurately, with complete deadliness.

I pulled the KGB agent into a linen closet and dropped him to the floor. The poison had paralyzed his diaphragm; an autopsy would probably show death by heart failure, unless the coroner happened to see the tiny hole in the man's right wrist. Even then, the poison I'd used was virtually undetectable. It'd require some sophisticated and complex chemical tests to find in the bloodstream. It didn't matter. By the time the body was

1

discovered, I'd be long gone, my mission accomplished.

The KGB agent doubled as a Russian diplomat and supposedly carried a tiny cylinder with microfilm inside. I searched his pockets, even checking the linings in the crisply starched whites he wore for his cover as a hospital orderly. I checked everywhere, but after twenty minutes of very thorough searching, I'd drawn a blank.

This job had turned a little sour; no matter what I did now, it wasn't going to be completely free of inquiry after I'd finished. I'd planned to let the man supplying the film leave the hospital before completing my mission, but this missed timing changed my schedule. That was a minor inconvenience.

It was now apparent that since the KGB agent didn't have the microfilm on him, Doctor Clayton Ducharme, Undersecretary for Middle Eastern Affairs in the U.S. State Department and part-time spy for the Soviets, still had it.

Slipping out into the corridor, I walked through the Bethesda, Maryland, Naval Hospital as if I belonged there. With top brass checking in all the time, security is very heavy, but no one paid attention to me. Over the years I've developed a knack akin to invisibility. People see me, then immediately disregard my presence. I always look as if I belong.

Outside the undersecretary's private room, I stopped and listened. His doctor and an assistant were examining the man. Slipping a piece of paper from my pocket, I made a few quick squiggles on it and went back to the nurses' station. I dropped the note and walked off.

Perfect.

Positioning myself outside Clayton Ducharme's door again, I waited until the loudspeaker in the hallway blared, "Doctor Goble to the Emergency Room," then watched as the doctor hurried out of Ducharme's room, followed by his assistant.

I brushed out nonexistent wrinkles in my white uniform and entered the room. No hospital door has a lock on it—no ward doors, at any rate—so I contented myself with sliding a chair up under the handle. Ducharme lounged in bed, smiling as he read the London *Times*. He didn't even look up as I crossed the spacious room.

"Doctor Clayton Ducharme?" I asked politely. He nodded, barely taking note of me. I was yet another in the faceless, nameless parade that poked and prodded him in an effort to cure his hernia. "The guy from the State Department?" Again a distracted nod. "The one selling classified material to the Soviets?"

That got his attention.

"What? What is this?" he demanded, dropping his paper to his lap and sitting up fully in bed. He winced slightly. His operation had been yesterday morning. Sharp gray eyes fastened on me, studying, analyzing, remembering.

I felt the full power of the man's commanding manner. He was used to power, to wielding it. Yet, he sensed that the power I controlled exceeded his, but egotism prevented the realization from sinking in. It was that same egotism that allowed a trusted member of the State Department to steal top-secret documents and sell them to the Russians. Clayton Ducharme didn't do it for money; my boss, David Hawk, had assured me Ducharme's finances were in stellar form. He could buy and sell the Hunt brothers on his worst day in the stock market. In a way, this immense wealth turned him into a spy.

Action. The thrill of espionage. Danger. Those were the keys to Ducharme's soul. Anything he wanted in the material world was his—fast cars, fast women, international travel. He'd even bought his fair share of excitement. Before taking the post in the State Department, he'd been one of the most famous big-game hunters in the world. But that had to pall. A .610 caliber Nitro Express against a charging elephant is an adrenaline rush, but only for a few seconds.

Clayton Ducharme, doctoral degree holder in political science from Princeton, multimillionaire, highly thought of member of Washington society, craved more.

He was going to get more than he bargained for.

"You can save us both a lot of trouble by giving me the microfilm," I said. I turned slightly, my left hand unbuttoning the bottom of my white orderly's tunic. My trusty Luger, Wilhelmina, rested within easy reach now, but using that noisy 9mm wasn't the way I wanted to go, not in the middle of a busy, crowded hospital. Still, I played this cautiously. Ducharme was no fool.

"I really don't know what you're talking about, young man. I recommend leaving immediately before I call the nurse."

"Yuceli Jettlow is dead," I said softly, my eyes locked with his. The muscles twitched around his eyes. Nothing else. I was glad I'd never played poker with this man. He'd be tremendous at bluffing. His contact gone, he had to know he was adrift and alone now, but he gave no sign other than the single involuntary muscle spasm.

"Jettlow is a minor functionary with the Soviet embassy," he said slowly. His eyes remained locked on mine; his brain shifted into high gear. He appraised, guessed, evaluated.

"He was a KGB agent," I corrected. I readied myself for response. My stiletto, Hugo, rested in a spring-loaded sheath on my right forearm. This was the way I'd play it. Knife. No sound. It didn't matter if Ducharme turned up dead as the result of an assassin. His death and Jettlow's would never be connected by those investigating. I wished I could have finished this assignment on schedule, letting Ducharme check out before removing him, but the failure to make the microfilm transfer at the appointed time ruined that.

"You're bluffing."

He saw from my expression that it was no bluff. A ripple of emotion crossed his face, a decision forming swiftly. He gave a curt, quick nod of his head.

"You're not bluffing," he said. "Very well, then. We can deal."

"The microfilm."

"The scandal caused by this minor indiscretion on my part would rock the Department. We both know that. I surrender the microfilm, you allow me to resign."

"The microfilm."

"Do we deal or does this get messy?" he snapped. Ducharme carried enough authority and power to always get his way in the past. "Look," he said in exasperation, "if you can't make the deal, contact your superior. Who is it? Denton? Horvat? If you're with the local FBI office, Horvat's your boss. I know him quite well. We can . . ." Realization hit him. "You're not FBI."

"AXE," I said.

He moved swiftly. I'd expected it and crossed the short distance between us before he got halfway out of bed. My hand locked on his brawny wrist and forced the small caliber automatic down. It discharged once, into his pillow. The tiny pop couldn't have been heard ten feet away. A quick twist, a sick crunching noise, and I broke his wrist. Moaning in pain, Ducharme turned and fell facedown on the bed.

"You son of a bitch. You broke it!"

"The microfilm."

"You've got a damned one-track mind." He turned over and glared, then sat up, obviously undecided whether to clutch his broken wrist or his belly where stitches had popped from the exertion.

"I've got a job to do."

"Jettlow was supposed to be here but didn't show up. Did you really kill him?" I didn't answer. He read it in my eyes. For the first time he realized the dangerous game he played had backfired. "Okay, we can trade," he said, obviously not wanting to understand. He thought he still had position, power. "In my shoe, in the closet. The left shoe sole comes away."

I backed to the closet, got the indicated shoe and quickly turned the sole. It came free enough to reveal a piece of microfilm almost two inches square. That much film could record just about every classified document in the State Department. I had no idea what the film contained, nor did I want to know.

"Any more?" I asked.

"That's it. Now call the FBI and tell Horvat to get his ass over here. I want to—"

My stiletto snapped into my hand. A quick under-hand toss lodged the needle-sharp point in Ducharme's throat. He reached up with his right hand, discovered the broken wrist didn't permit any dexterity, and then died, surprise still etched on his handsome face. Tiny flecks of blood had spattered up to his graying temples, but other than this it was a clean kill, swift, painless. It was more than he deserved.

Hawk had ordered me to recover the microfilm and stop the leak. Permanently.

I'd accomplished my mission, even if it had been im-provised at the last minute due to the timing mix-ups on the KGB's part. That wasn't like them, but accidents do happen.

Retrieving Hugo, I wiped the blade on a tissue from the box on the bedside table, straightened my tunic again and left.

Doctor Goble and his assistant orbited back into the corridor as I went to the elevator. As the elevator doors closed in front of me, I heard the commotion begin. They'd found their ex-patient.

TWO

David Hawk sat behind his broad oak desk, a half-smoked cigar clamped in the corner of his mouth. The cigar had gone out almost fifteen minutes ago. He didn't seem to notice, and I wasn't about to tell him. The blue, clinging smoke from that stogey was enough to choke me. Hawk debriefed me on the mission I'd just completed, not too happy about my eliminating Clayton Ducharme in the manner I'd chosen. It caused inquiry. AXE existed on the fringes of the government, a super-secret organization accountable only to the President of the United States.

My eyes kept drifting over to the red telephone at the edge of Hawk's desk less than an arm's length away. All he had to do was pick up the phone and the President, wherever he was in the world, answered within minutes. Hawk carried the burden of knowing that the phone worked the other way, too. If the President had a particularly sensitive mission, he never hesitated letting Hawk know.

"You could have waited, N3," he chided.

"I'm sorry, no, sir, I couldn't. If Ducharme had left the hospital with the microfilm, this presented new opportunities to pass it along to another KGB agent. I decided recovering the film was more important than not causing a stir."

"It's done that," he said glumly. "Seen the evening news?"

I had.

"Well, it'll cool off after a while. There wasn't any mention of Jettlow, at least. But the Russians know what happened."

"It's too bad Villareal wasn't their pickup agent," I said. I'd wanted to take out the Cuban agent for some time, both for professional and personal reasons. He worked closely with the KGB and, on occasion, performed more brilliantly than they did. Villareal was a worthy opponent and whoever permanently removed him would be doing the Free World a big favor.

"The Cubans couldn't care less about the data on this microfilm. Tell me, N3, do you know what's on it?" Hawk tapped the tiny square of film with his index finger. The question surprised me. I looked more carefully at my boss. He wasn't accusing me of illicit knowledge; that would have been a violation of my orders and ordinary conduct in the field. I didn't have the need to know, and it really didn't interest me greatly one way or the other. A highly placed State Department diplomat had turned traitor; that was all I needed to know.

Hawk's rhetorical question had more ominous overtones to it than accusing me of sneaking a peek. His face betrayed nothing, except a little too much strain and desk work. Small dark circles formed under his eyes and his chin carried the beginnings of a dewlap. Still, for a man almost thirty years my elder, he kept in good form.

"Should I know the contents?" I asked.

"This microfilm contains all the documents pertaining to the Afghanistan invasion by the Russians, their guerrilla activities against Pakistan and India, as well as up-to-the-minute reports on how the Mujeheddin are faring."

"Mujeheddin?"

"The Afghanistan rebels. Name means Holy Warrior. For a ragtag band of starving peasants, they've done surprisingly well against the Soviets. One account here," again he tapped the microfilm for emphasis, "tells of their rather remarkable efforts in the Panjshir Valley, about forty miles north of Kabul. The Soviets had about fifteen thousand troops, fifteen hundred armored vehicles, their usual air support from helicopter gunships. What had started out as a swift attack turned into a siege. Weeks dragged on and the Russians finally backed off. Only one thousand Mujeheddin turned back fifteen times their number. It seems that the Mujeheddin gained considerable amounts of Soviet arms and equipment from this ill-conceived venture on the Russians' part."

"The Russians still haven't taken the Panjshir Valley?" I asked, surprised. The Russian troops were well-trained and equipped with the best the Kremlin could provide. But then our troops in Vietnam had had the same advantages.

"No. The official TASS news releases, of course, state a smashing victory and all that, but it's not true. They've taken to booby-trapping the rebel countryside, dropping those plastic gadgets—what are they called?"

"Butterflies," I supplied.

"Yes, butterflies, and hope that the Afghani guerrillas pick them up. More children than adults are being killed. This only stiffens the Mujeheddin's resolve."

"Ducharme stole some interesting information," I said. "But the Russians know all this, and we didn't release it to the press."

"True, N3," Hawk said. The cigar shifted to the other corner of his mouth. He did it in such a way that he used his tongue; both hands remained on his desktop. "What the Russians don't know is the identity of the rebel leader—Massoud is his name—or his contacts with our intelligence gathering people."

"He wants us to aid him?" It was the same old story.

"No, really the Mujeheddin don't want *any* outside interference, U.S. or Soviet. But they do want aid in the form of weapons and supplies, especially medical supplies. This is a primitive region, a hard one with little food and scant creature comforts."

The pieces began falling into place. Or so I thought.

"This Massoud is trading information for supplies?"

"Yes. The entire Afghanistan operation has been a

disaster for the Russians, yet they don't give any indication of pulling out. They seem willing to remain for as long as it takes, which may be decades. The Afghanis have thrown out the British twice in the past hundred years. The Russians are just another foreign invader to them."

"What do the Soviets want?"

"Pakistan, and then India."

"What?"

Hawk looked grim as he picked up the microfilm and inserted it into a slot on his desk. A map of the world on the far wall folded back to reveal a projection screen. The microfilm went through a series of lenses and the contents came out large enough for easy viewing.

"Here it is, Nick." Hawk rarely used my given name—unless he was being very confidential. "The complete Soviet plan for the invasion of Pakistan and India. It's been done before, going through the Khyber Pass. The distance between Kabul and the Khyber is only two hundred miles, but it's all desert and the Mujeheddin remain in control outside the large cities. The Soviets hoped to break the rebel strength with the Panjshir Valley campaign. Instead, it pushed them down even further and set back their timetable."

"Why do they want Pakistan? It's not much of a country, all things considered. Millions of mouths to feed, and the Russians have had four bad grain crops in a row. They're having trouble supplying their own people, much less the Eastern Bloc countries. Adding Pakistan to their satellites now is suicidal."

"True, but the Russians are intent on having a warm water shipping port. Much of their history is geared toward such a goal. And they've consistently failed. Why they chose this particular time to go through the Afghanistan Door, I can't say, but the idea of a port for their shipping that doesn't freeze over most of the year is a national obsession and has been since Peter the Great."

"Afghanistan Door?"

"The Khyber Pass. The Scythians, Persians, Greeks,

Seljuks, Tartars, Mongols and Duranis have all successfully invaded the subcontinent of India through this single pass. The Russians want to add their name to the long list."

"They don't know how much of their plans we've discovered, is that it?"

"Exactly. Clayton Ducharme would have given the Soviets information it's taken us two years and twelve agents to collect, not to mention arms and medical shipments to Massoud. As long as they think we're in the dark, they'll take their time and prepare a cautious, safe route through the Khyber Pass."

"You mean consolidate Afghanistan, then go for Pakistan and India."

"Just that. It is to our advantage, then, to prevent such a takeover in Afghanistan. With or without aid being supplied by Egypt and China, the Mujeheddin are doing well."

"You mentioned guerrillas a few minutes ago, but it sounded like you meant the Russians. I don't understand."

"It's here in Massoud's information. They planned on softening up the area by infiltrating guerrilla units of their own. A few units of guerrillas through the Khyber Pass and the Mujeheddin can be blamed. Some appropriate destruction, the reflexive pulling back of Pakistani troops, then the big push."

"World opinion . . ." I began.

"In face of a warm water port, world opinion seems nothing to the leaders in the Kremlin. I said this was an obsession; it's more. It's a *huge* obsession."

"Enough to risk World War III over?"

Hawk snorted and, for the first time, noticed his cigar wasn't lit. He struck a wooden match, held the charred cigar tip to the flame and inhaled deeply. Blue smoke curled up. I shook my head, got out my cigarette case and indulged in one of my few vices. The gold-tipped monogrammed cigarettes inside were specially made of the finest Turkish blends; to smoke one was a sensory experience.

"N3, the risk of nuclear war is always great. Still, I doubt the President would press the button over Pakistan. Short of actual attack on the continental United States, I doubt if the button would ever be pressed. That's a final decision, a terminal one for not only the U.S. but most of the world. The Soviets know there is a risk of war. They've cold-bloodedly calculated that we will not launch an atomic strike if they invade Pakistan."

"The actual decision about an invasion of Pakistan is in the microfilm Ducharme stole?"

"Yes, of course it is. The Russians would *know* rather than guess our reaction with this set of documents. They'd know exactly what we've found out. They can guess, they can sweat, but they don't know right now."

I was sorry I hadn't eliminated Doctor Ducharme in a more painful way. He had been a dilettante dabbling in espionage. That ennui of his could have meant the deaths of millions.

"So the Russians soften up the Khyber Pass area with guerrillas while they continue to use their regular Army units against the Afghani Mujeheddin," I said, thinking out loud, trying to get it all straight. "The Mujeheddin are, for the moment, doing well enough against them to keep them at bay. We've got some time to sway Pakistan into believing that the U.S.S.R. really is going to invade. But proof of this is needed."

"You are to go to Afghanistan, Pakistan, wherever seems best for the purpose, N3, and obtain concrete proof that the Soviets are adventuring into Pakistan and plan an invasion through the Khyber Pass."

"Anything else?" I said, blowing smoke out into the air. I watched it lazily combine with the heavier blue from Hawk's cigar.

"Stopping a major war should be enough," said Hawk, "but we'd like a little more from you."

"Recon work?"

"Exactly. Our agents in the area are too widely spaced for effective work. You'll be going in alone—cover of your choice—and getting all the intelligence you can, both on the Russians and the people of the area."

"I'll get right on it."

Hawk didn't even look up. He'd already turned off the projector and retrieved the microfilm from the slot in his desk. The film went into an envelope and was dropped into a drawer. He started to say something further to me when the red telephone rang. He took a deep breath and picked it up.

I left, glad all I had to do was stop a war. No incentive in the world could have made me take over Hawk's job in that instant.

THREE

I left the AXE offices on Dupont Circle and walked swiftly away, not bothering with a taxi, even though the Washington, D.C., sky was lead-gray and ready to open up with a torrential spring downpour. I had to think. Hawk had given me a free hand in setting up my cover. Whatever I wanted would be arranged, but the best and safest cover was one I had a part in establishing.

I knew little enough about Pakistan and that area of the world, but decided this country was the best point of entry. Spending most of the afternoon in AXE's extensive library had convinced me that I was right. For a few rupees anything could be bought—except loyalty. Pakistan was officially a military dictatorship, but life in that country wasn't too restricted. In addition, everyone knows his place in a dictatorship and buying officials is a way of life. Who knows? They might even be honest crooks—staying bought.

Sheep and the wool from them, a few skins, rugs and that was it for legal export from Pakistan. On the more pragmatic and illegal side, hashish and raw opium provided about eighty percent of the country's real export profit.

Enter Nick Carter, master drug dealer.

The clouds that had promised rain finally delivered. I turned up the collar on my coat and walked a little faster. I hoped this wasn't an omen for my mission.

* * *

"Coke?" the bartender asked.

"Not interested," I replied. "I'm looking for something a lot heavier."

"Heavier?" A look of concern crossed his thin features. He shook his head, almost dislodging a lock of hair greased down with a vile-smelling ointment. "Can't do it. Not here, buddy."

"Here," I said, leaning across the bar and sliding my fingers around the collar of his shirt. I tightened my grip and twisted, knuckles driving into his Adam's apple. He sputtered and tried to step back. I applied more pressure and lifted him up onto his toes. "I've been told this is the place I want. Let's talk, shall we?"

A hard, cold shape nudged me in the right kidney. I didn't have to be told it was a gun, a very large caliber one. The bouncer had seen what happened to the bartender and had come over to lend a little sadistic assistance.

"Don't hassle Jimmy none, mister," came the command from behind. A harder jab of the pistol accentuated the request.

I released the bartender and sat back down in my chair, the gun still prodding into my body.

"Take it easy unless you want to eat it," I said.

Jimmy looked shocked, then frightened. His hand went to his bruised throat. If given a clear space, he'd turn rabbit and run. Trapped behind the bar, all he could do was look increasingly terrified. Obviously no one had spoken to the bouncer like this before.

Looking sidelong, I saw why. This guy's neck size and IQ were about the same. I smiled, and that confused him. Fear was the only acceptable—and expected —reaction.

In that instant, I moved faster than a striking cobra. My hand flashed down and grabbed the paw holding the .45 automatic. I lifted, twisted, then shoved down hard. The motion caught his finger in the trigger guard while preventing him from being able to squeeze off the round and ventilate my precious body. I kept the pressure on, kept twisting, kept pressing my luck. I drove the bouncer to his knees. When the thick finger finally broke, I jerked the gun away.

"You bastard," he said. The pain slowly filtered through to his walnut-sized brain.

My punch drove less than six inches and went straight for the exposed bull-neck. He choked, gasped, turned purple, then vomited. I got out of the way in time.

"Mister, you don't wanna know what he's gonna do to you when . . ." The bartender's eyes had gone saucer-large and his chin quivered. "He's killed men, mister."

"Yeah," I said. I took out the clip from the .45 and pocketed it, then jacked out the shell in the chamber. I dropped the heavy automatic on the floor beside the weakly heaving giant. "Learn to use this thing," I said to him, "so you won't hurt yourself."

Starting out, I felt eyes on me from all quarters. The hairs on the back of my neck prickled, waiting for the bullet to blow my brains out, to sever my spine, to spatter my blood all over. Nothing. I relaxed a little. My goal was almost achieved.

"You," came the command from the back of the bar. My hand rested on the doorknob. I said nothing. Then, "Let's talk."

Morey Swearingen was a kingpin in the drug trafficking underworld. I'd gotten through to him in the only way he understood. Roughing up the bouncer had been a risk, but it'd paid off.

"Why?" I asked, not turning. "All I'm getting here is static. I can go home and get that from my old lady."

"You'll get your damn teeth kicked in if you don't get your ass back here."

I looked around. Swearingen hardly looked the tough guy, yet his files were almost an inch thick with various crimes. He'd started off as a teen-aged numbers runner in New York, worked his way up to hit man accounting for no fewer than four syndicate executions, then branched out into prostitution and eventually drugs, running those operations on his own instead of working for others. His brother-in-law was a big man with the labor unions. Together, they formed a drug smuggling ring with worldwide connections.

"You?" I said, laughing. Morey Swearingen was a thin man, slightly built, and looked more like a corporate accountant. "You'll do the kicking?"

"You want to talk or deal?" he asked.

I went back to the table. Swearingen drank only Perrier and lime. I remembered from his dossier that he was a teetotaler, an ulcer almost causing him to bleed to death internally three years ago. While he had a tendency to pamper himself, the man had few other weaknesses. Standing over him like a mountain, I said nothing.

"Sit."

I sat.

"You wanted something harder than coke. I heard what you told Jimmy. What you interested in? Smack?"

"How do you know I'm not a cop?" I asked.

His eyes darted to the dark form on the barroom floor. The bouncer stirred and lifted himself onto hands and knees. He shook like a leaf in a high wind.

"Nobody does that to Rico," he said. "He's going to kill you, whether you're a cop or not."

"I'm scared."

"You ought to be." He took a sip of his drink, peering at me over the lime stuck to the rim of the glass.

"How do you know I'm not a cop?" I repeated.

"You don't have the stink about you. It's the way they walk, everything. You're not the heat."

I smiled and said, "Let's do a real deal."

"You don't want to buy?"

"I want to buy *for* you. In Pakistan. Go to the supplier, get the opium direct, score some hash, do it right. Cut out all the middlemen. Your profits would go up— five, six hundred percent."

"Vertical integration?"

Morey Swearingen surprised me. He talked like an accountant. Crime had changed character drastically in recent years. While the bully boys like Rico still existed, the top men in organized crime had become more educated, smarter, more sophisticated. The training ground for real crime today had become the graduate schools of business. I bet Swearingen even held sinking fund debentures and tax free municipals in his portfolio.

"Something like that. I buy direct in Pakistan, arrange for the refining; your brother-in-law handles the shipping; and you do the merchandising."

"You know a goddamn lot about my business. Why should I listen to you? Rico wants to snuff you out. Why shouldn't I let him?"

Rico leaned heavily against the bar. His face was a pasty white and he gasped hard even as he wiped off his chin. It'd be another few minutes before he became a rabid animal again.

"You'd lose out on a lot of money."

He sighed and shook his head.

"You want me to bankroll this scheme. No."

"I have the money," I said. "I want your connections."

"You have the money? How much?"

"Five million," I said. That got Swearingen's attention. "And for risking it, I want to be damn sure I'm onto a reliable source of raw opium. You've got the connections over there. I'll feed the refined smack through to you and we can all make some good coin."

"What are you looking to make out of this?"

"Triple my money," I said. "Inside six months."

"If you've got that kind of bread, why bother with me? Go for it yourself. It's not that hard establishing yourself in Pakistan. Those wogs will do anything for an American buck."

"That'd take months," I said honestly. "I want to turn the money fast. Also, I don't have any pull with the customs people in this country. I don't want the hassle of distribution; you've already got the machinery set up for that."

"Yeah," Swearingen said, obviously considering every angle. If he saw any way, he'd do me out of the five million and leave me dead. All I cared about was convincing him to contact his people in Pakistan and tell them I was okay.

Rico coughed a couple more times and grabbed a

glass of whiskey from Jimmy's shaking hand. The giant downed the liquor so fast it made my throat burn thinking about it. I doubted the booze was anything more than rotgut. A tremor earthquaked through the man mountain, then he settled down. He was getting dangerous again.

"Where'd you get five mil?" Swearingen asked.

"I saved my pennies," I said sarcastically. "My financial backers are not interested in having their names bandied about."

"I don't deal unless I know everything."

"Let's just say that my principals aren't very happy with the way the stock market's been going lately and want to turn a profit on their investments."

"Or let's say you represent some hotshot corporate manager who's in trouble over a bit of creative bookkeeping and needs a hell of a lot of money to keep from having his ass thrown in jail for embezzlement." This was exactly what I'd hoped Swearingen would think. I looked a little crestfallen to add credence to his theorizing.

"Five million is easy for him to come by—for a short while. He needs a lot more to cover losses," I said, as if admitting everything. "If this goes through, though, there'll be ample opportunity to borrow another five million, maybe more."

Morey Swearingen thought about all the angles. If the deal went sour, he wasn't out any money. If it worked, he had a pipeline to corporate America and an inexhaustible supply of capital. At worst, he stood a good chance of blackmailing the chief financial officer so foolhardy with his company's precious money. Swearingen couldn't lose on this, no matter what happened.

"I think we can deal," he finally said.

"I'll be in touch," I told him. I got up, went to the bar where Rico finally focused his eyes, saw the hatred there, then measured my punch. I wound up for this one. The roundhouse swing came from far back. Even with my feet squarely planted, the impact of my fist in Rico's solar plexus knocked me off balance.

It knocked him out.

I left, never looking back. The first step to closing the Afghan Door had been taken.

FOUR

I'd flown into Islamabad on Swiss Air, gotten through customs without a hitch, then boarded an ancient narrow-gauge train for Lahore. My dealings with Morey Swearingen had gone smoothly, and I'd never seen Rico again after our last encounter. I had the feeling Swearingen held him in reserve, in case I tried to double-cross him. Swearingen had furnished the names of dealers in raw opium and had promised to telex them with information about our new plans. I chose Achmed Kohar as the most likely source for the information I needed. Kohar dealt outside of Lahore, in the city of Mughalpura, and had connections throughout the country, especially ones reaching up into the Khyber Pass area.

I played all this by ear. A trip to the region was no doubt in the cards for me, so I wanted as much information about Soviet activity there as possible. I also needed to know about native resistance, how much those on the Pakistan side of the border aided the Mujeheddin, what the chances were for stirring up anti-Soviet feelings. In a way, this was work the CIA should have been doing, but Hawk had explained the problem. The CIA was under close scrutiny for their part in Latin American politics and had to pull back from covert activities in many places around the world. On the surface, all my assignment amounted to was information gathering. If my findings were positive enough, I was to attempt to stir up peasant resistance against the Russians.

If I were really lucky, I might throw a monkey wrench into Soviet designs on the region for years to come.

The train rattled and rolled until I began to feel a little seasick. I stared out at the countryside, glad I only passed through. Stark, barren, the semi-arid brown plains didn't look capable of growing anything, much less the small sprouts of green on the areas under cultivation. Less than twenty percent of the country was under cultivation; the thin, rocky soil couldn't support much in the way of agriculture. And about three-quarters of what there was out there had to be irrigated.

But the farmland wasn't the country's big attraction. In the far distance to the north rose the tail end of the Hindu Kush. The immense mountain chain ran through the length of Afghanistan and into Pakistan. The Panjshir Valley nestled itself squarely in the middle of the Hindu Kush. I'd probably never see that region, but this was sight enough for me. Back home in the U.S. the people living in Colorado don't call anything under fourteen thousand feet a mountain. Here, a tiny little hillock started there. The big mountains really shot into the stratosphere. The distant mountains, cloaked in the purple haze of immense distance, were young, folded and heavily faulted. Sharp edges showed even from the rattling, clanking railway car with its dirty windows and smoky interior.

A woman carrying a small child and dragging along a pair of chickens on a leash collapsed into the seat across from me. I was glad I'd chosen to ride first class.

I leaned back in the uncomfortable seat and tried to relax. In spite of the discomfort, the growing heat and stench inside the car, and the incredible din of wheels on narrow-gauge track, I slept all the way into Lahore.

"Sahib," came the polite inquiry, accompanied by a tug at my sleeve. I jerked free and turned, not liking anyone to touch me. The man was only a few inches shorter than I was, solidly built, had a long head, fair skin and eyes so blue any Swede would have envied

them. "I am to take you to my master."

"Achmed Kohar?"

He bowed, touching fingers to lips and forehead.

"My master is most anxious to meet with you. Come. A car awaits."

A sixth sense made me uneasy. "Give me the directions. I must contact my . . . principals. Tell them that everything is going along just fine." The reaction was as expected. The man stiffened slightly, the tiny muscle movements betraying him long before he acted.

I punched him directly in the stomach, catching him as he fell. An ornately engraved knife with a seven-inch blade clattered to the train station platform. I kicked the knife beneath the wheels of the train, but fast as I was, many had seen. Urchins dived under the train to retrieve the valuable weapon, not caring for their own safety. Even as they fought over the knife, the train began to move.

Sickened, I watched helplessly as one child, perhaps no more than ten or eleven, lost a hand under the wheels reaching for the knife. This split second of divided attention on my part allowed the man to recover and act. Powerful arms locked around my body and lifted my feet off the floor. He swung me around, intent on throwing me under the train wheels. Infuriated that my carelessness made this possible, and that all those watching took it so casually, I found new strength.

I kicked and fought free. Again he tried to shove me off the platform and under the train. My reaction came automatically. I trapped the wrist, gave it a mighty turn and sent the gasping man somersaulting outward. He crashed hard into the side of the moving train and slid down onto the tracks.

He screamed once before he died.

I spun and walked off, my bag in hand. Even before I threw the man to his death, I saw three others homing in on me like hunting dogs. I hadn't had time to question the man and now regretted it. A part of me feared that the KGB had been alerted and had already sent killers to remove me from the game. Another part said that rival opium dealers often fought for world markets. Their tactics were crude and vicious. If Kohar were in the throes of such a war, I was caught dead center.

Outside the station, I jumped into the last taxi in line. The drivers in front screamed out in anger, waving fists and shouting curses in Urdu, maligning my mother.

"Hotel Dennison," I said to the driver. He smiled, broken, yellowed teeth showing through dark lips.

"At once!" he cried, wheeling around the others. If they hadn't relented and gotten out of his way, he'd have run over them.

"First time in Lahore, eh?" he called back. The engine missed on at least two of its four cylinders; I doubted the car had any brakes at all; and the peculiar lurching spelled trouble for the suspension. Still, it took me away from the men on the train platform.

"It shows?" I asked.

"Oh, no, *sahib,* no!" he lied. "You look like you were born here."

As we rattled along, I watched the pedestrians closely. Many were of the same ethnic stock of the would-be killer at the train station: Pathan. Others were shorter, stockier, more Arabic blood flowing in their veins. All looked underfed and willing to kill their grandmothers for a decent meal.

"I'm looking for a particular shop," I said.

"You don't want to go to the hotel?"

"Maybe the shop first," I said, as if changing my mind. I'd called out the name of one of the hotels I knew in Lahore in case anyone at the train station overheard. That might keep the trio bird-dogging me on the go long enough for me to make my rendezvous with the drug wholesaler. "A shop specializing in brass vases, things like that." Morey Swearingen had told me to contact the clerk in a store known as the Brass Cage; he hadn't known the address. From here I was to make contact with Achmed Kohar. The man at the train station had given himself away by not mentioning a change in plans. He'd assumed an American would jump at the chance of avoiding all the squalor and press of people and that removing me would be that much easier.

"All shops are in special areas," said the driver. "Takes special knowledge to find the proper *mohalla*."

"What's that?"

"A trade district. Look down this alley. A *mohalla* specializing in skins." The stench of uncured hides made me clamp my teeth firmly together. "In the other direction, a *mohalla* of goat cheese." I lucked out this time; the wind blew from the rotting goat skins past me and kept away the souring milk odors.

"My friend recommended a specific store—the Brass Cage." The driver stiffened, his hands clamping down hard on the battered steering wheel.

"You want to go there?"

"I just said I did."

The sudden acceleration pushed me back into the cushions. The driver's narrow escapes from death on both left and right became even more harrowing. He finally slammed on the brakes, skidded to a halt and motioned down a dark, garbage-strewn alley.

"Down there."

I paid him and watched him rocket away. The Brass Cage obviously had a reputation transcending most stores. Either that or the driver didn't want to be mixed up in a local gang war. I picked my way down the center of the alley, cautiously avoiding the larger heaps of debris. By now, my nose rejected all unsavory odors, my sense of smell totally paralyzed. The people lining the streets were either beggars rattling tin cups at me or merchants interested only in dragging me inside their particular shop to fleece an unwitting tourist blundering along their alley. I avoided both, seeking out my contact point. Halfway down the *mohalla* of brass merchants I saw a crudely lettered sign in Urdu, Arabic and English. This was Achmed Kohar's shop.

Inside the store presented a world of change from outside. Soft incenses robbed the odors of their bite, music seeped from behind lavish tapestries hung around the room and the light level never varied from twilight.

The clerk spoke rapidly in what I took to be Urdu.

I answered in Arabic.

He shifted to English, saying, "You speak well, sir. How may this humble clerk assist you?"

"I'd like to purchase a few items to take home with me."

"Your wives will be overjoyed at your generosity. May the selections from this modest store not offend you too greatly."

I looked around at the brass and copper goods, finding myself momentarily taken by both the cheap prices and high quality. My attention moved from the wares to three men in the street outside the shop. The trio must have known exactly where I headed to have gotten here so fast from the train station. They stood in the middle of the street arguing among themselves. The smallest one gestured toward the door, wanting to make a full frontal assault.

"Tell me," I said, turning back to the clerk, "if you know of Achmed Kohar."

"Kohar?" he asked, his face impassive.

"I've been referred to him by a mutual friend in the States."

"Who might this mutual friend be, sir?"

"Morey Swearingen," I said. "He told me to pass along the latest baseball scores." This served as a recognition code. "I'd prefer to do this as quickly as possible."

The three men burst into the shop, knives drawn.

The clerk's expression never changed. For a single sinking instant I wondered if I'd gone from the frying pan into the fire—that he and the three were all on the same side. My hand tugged at Wilhelmina, freeing the Luger and getting the safety off for quick action. Even with my trusty friend, three—four?—against one made for lousy odds.

The staccato *ack-ack-ack* of a machine gun echoed through the shop; the clerk's expression remained impassive at the carnage wrought. The three men straightened and were tossed back into the wall, dancing like marionettes on a string. Only when the machine gun fell silent did they slip down the wall, leaving bloody tracks and cracked plaster behind. They slumped into one another, all quite dead.

The incense covered the smell of death. The soft music began playing once again.

"Your weapon is not required. My master is most interested in finding out how your Dodgers are doing this season after their World Series win last year."

I looked from the emotionless clerk to the three dead men and back. He wasn't kidding . . . about anything.

"I think I'm going to enjoy meeting your master."

Silent men came out from behind the tapestry hangings and began removing the corpses and cleaning up the mess.

I'd made my contact in Lahore.

FIVE

We left by the back door, going into another alley no different from the one in front of the store. I wondered if the bodies would be disposed of by simply being tossed onto one of the garbage heaps along the alley. Probably. What Pakistan lacked in sanitation, it more than made up for in convenience.

"Sir, a poor conveyance to take you to my master." The clerk bowed deeply and indicated a Mercedes 600 limousine at the mouth of the alley. The stark contrast between such luxury and the grinding poverty all around struck me hard. It wasn't anything I hadn't seen in other parts of the world; still, it rocked me. It always does.

I got in and entered a different world. The darkened windows cut off the view of the interior as we drove silently away. A soft, air-conditioned breeze caressed my face and took away some of the sweat forming due to the stifling heat in the city; the glass wall separating the chauffeur and the rear compartment where I sat made me feel as if I floated in some dimensionless limbo.

Peering out the windows, I got some idea where we headed. Lahore quickly vanished and the barren countryside appeared. From the angle and location of the sun, we headed in the right direction for Mughalpura. I'd had enough run-ins with the opposition, whoever they were. Dealing with the right people would prove sticky enough for my taste. I had to walk a tightwire, dangling the promise of immense wealth in front of

Kohar to loosen his tongue about conditions in the Khyber Pass region, while convincing him I was as dishonest as he was. If he thought he could make off with the full five million I'd mentioned to Swearingen back in Washington, I had no doubt Achmed Kohar would try killing me.

To arrange for five million dollars' worth of raw opium was hazardous all by itself. The rest of my mission paled in comparison.

The chauffeur smoothly turned down a paved road, keeping us well away from the city I thought to be Mughalpura. We drove into the "suburbs." He finally braked and stopped, getting out to open the door for me.

For an instant, I stood and gaped. I'd thought to tempt and entice Kohar with the promise of riches.

He lived in a mansion beyond the wildest opium dreams of poet Samuel Taylor Coleridge when he wrote about Kubla Khan's pleasure dome in fabled Xanadu.

"Mister Carter, welcome to my humble dwelling," came an effusive voice. A man dressed in a natty three-piece business suit, more appropriate for a bank president than a Pakistani dope dealer, came out, arms extended. He hugged me, kissed me on both cheeks and generally did a good job of checking me for weapons in the process. "Do come in."

"This is a remarkable place. A palace," I said. I didn't have to feign enthusiasm. I meant it. This "humble dwelling" looked even more out of place amid the tumble-down shacks I'd seen along the road leading to it. A fifteen-foot wall surrounded the estate, like oyster shells protecting the pearl within. Vast marble columns rose up from the house proper, a decided Arabic flair to the architecture.

"The dome is a convex Bengal roof," Achmed Kohar said proudly. "A most difficult thing to build."

"The Shah Jahan built a fort using it. The Naulakha Pavilion, I believe."

Kohar looked at me strangely, then said, "It is unusual for one of your country to know the history of this poor part of the world. The magnificence left by the Shah Jahan is not normally part of your history class."

"A little hobby of mine," I said, laying the ground-work for questions I'd ask later. "I've always been fasci-nated by the Khyber Pass, Afghanistan, Pakistan."

"An odd hobby for one who deals in the commodity mentioned by Mister Swearingen."

"Not all U.S. gangsters are like Morey," I answered.

"I have found him to be honest in our dealings. He is a worthy businessman."

"As I am. We shall get along well, I'm sure."

"We will, if you can answer one question."

I tensed, wondering what was coming. Kohar's body-guards lined the hall we'd entered. Any two of them looked more than a match for me. They carried Ingram submachine guns slung over their shoulders—and there were no fewer than ten of the guards in sight. One in particular eyed me coldly. I didn't have to be a Tarot card reader to know at least that many more were within easy call.

"What do you want to know?"

"Do you think the Dodger pitching staff is as good as last year's team?"

I didn't know whether to laugh or cry.

My eyes widened in shock at the sight.

"Impressive, isn't it?" Kohar said, knowing that it was. "I have weighed in at least fourteen hundred pounds of hashish in the past month. This is what re-mains. Perhaps five hundred pounds."

The mound was head high and extended back a full arm's reach. I couldn't even begin to guess what the Drug Enforcement Agency team would think knowing I'd come this close to high-quality hash.

"But you are not interested in this. You wish to deal in more valuable areas. Like this."

Stacked against the inside of the protective wall around the well-tended garden was a mound of raw opi-um that took my breath away. Fully ten feet high, it reached back along the wall a distance of fifty feet. My mind tried to calculate how much heroin this could be refined into; the numbers all ran into the millions of dollars and hundreds of pounds.

"Seven tons of raw opium. Here. Now. We can deal for it whenever you wish."

"Seven tons," I said. "Never seen that much before."

Achmed laughed and slapped me on the back. I winced at the blow. His hand had heavy calluses on it that hadn't gotten there by merely counting his money.

"I am the top dealer in all of Pakistan."

"You have any trouble with rival organizations?" I asked, thinking of the men pursuing me. I wanted them positively identified as drug traffickers and not KGB agents, although the two were often one and the same.

"The current situation is none of your concern."

"Four men came after me the instant I got off the train in Lahore. That's not something I want to live with while I'm in your country."

"They did represent a disgruntled group of investors," he said, sounding quite a bit like Morey Swearingen. "A small *pakhtunwali*, a blood feud, has resulted from their disapproval of the way we did business."

I translated that into real English: a rival group had been cheated by Kohar and now wanted to kill anyone dealing with him. I also did a bit more translating. Someone in Kohar's tight little group had supplied the information about my arrival.

"Then it doesn't matter. I just wanted to be sure they weren't Russians."

"Russians?" he asked, startled. "Why would they have any dealings with me? Their government is so prudish." He laughed harshly, then lowered his voice to a conspiratorial whisper. "And they are some of my best customers."

"How's that?"

"Their troops in Afghanistan smoke much hashish. They trade it for weapons, ammunition, things I find remarkably profitable trading in Lahore and elsewhere."

"They aren't also in the market for the opium, are they?" I had to keep up the facade of wanting the tons of raw opium for myself.

"No, it is too sophisticated for the Russian soldiers," he assured me.

"You deal much in the Khyber Pass area? That must be how you get the stuff over into Afghanistan."

"Some dealings in that region," he admitted. "You aren't thinking of going into business with the *kafirs* who met you at the train?"

"No, nothing like that," I said. "I'm just curious about the Russians. Guess all Americans are. They're our bogeyman."

"Bogeyman?"

"Demon," I said. "Also, I wouldn't want all this fine opium to be overrun if they should happen to invade through the Khyber Pass. You yourself said they were puritanical. They'd burn this entire place, if they came into Pakistan."

I watched Kohar carefully. His face hardened when I mentioned the possibility of Soviet invasion. It wasn't the first time he'd heard about it, of that I was certain. I kept pumping, probing, prodding. And bit by bit Kohar supplied me with the information.

"There's no chance of them doing that, is there?" I asked again as we walked toward the mansion.

"They'll come through the Khyber Pass soon enough, intent on Pakistan," he said, spitting. "But we Moslems will never yield. And you will have all the opium you desire."

As we entered the cooler interior, I saw one of Kohar's guards watching me, the one who had been especially hostile at my arrival. He turned and quickly left. The expression on his face hadn't been one of suspicion as much as it had been one of recognition. This close to the Soviet Union, the KGB had to have men infiltrated everywhere. A major drug dealer like Kohar presented them with as good an opportunity to gather intelligence as it did me.

"I need some rest," I said. "Besides, it is nearly time for your afternoon prayers."

"You are not Moslem." The sentence came out carrying multiple meaning. It was an accusation, a question, an invitation to become a convert.

"No." I heard the caller begin the call to the faithful. Kohar bowed and left. Instead of entering my room, I followed the man who had spotted me. Somehow I doubted he unrolled a prayer rug and faced Mecca.

I was right.

He bent over a small but powerful radio rig, speaking softly and swiftly in Russian. I eavesdropped for a moment to get the gist of what he reported. It boiled down to what Kohar had already told me. The Soviet invasion through the Khyber Pass and into Pakistan was scheduled to begin within weeks. He relayed what I had been asking, gave a brief physical description of me that didn't do my vanity any good and then started to give his opinions. I broke off the antenna just as he uttered the codename: N3.

He whirled, his fists searching for a soft spot in my belly. I tensed and he found only granite-hard muscle. The antenna I'd broken off was a flexible whip. I lashed out and caught him beside the head. When he reacted to the searing pain, I drove my elbow up under his chin. The sudden snap told me I'd broken his neck.

I checked the radio frequency he'd used and decided this transmission went over the mountains and into Afghanistan. The KGB directorate might not act for days on the scanty information he'd sent before I silenced him. Their bureaucrats are even worse than ours about tackling unusual situations. The radioman on duty in Afghanistan might even report a full transmission, if this had been a regularly scheduled broadcast.

I tinkered inside the radio, making sure no one else could use it, then hid it and the body under a rug in the corner of the room. They'd both be found, but maybe not for some time.

I hoped to report in and be out of Kohar's palace before the afternoon prayers were completed. But I'd have to hurry.

SIX

The body would be found all too soon. I had to be long gone before Achmed Kohar decided he wanted revenge. It wouldn't matter that the guard had been a double agent working for the KGB and that he had probably sold out Kohar's deepest, darkest secrets to the other side in the current scuffle over drug territory. All Kohar knew were blood feuds and holy wars and dying.

He could die any time he wanted. I intended to go on living for a long, long time.

Back in my quarters, I hastily opened the suitcase and stripped out the lining. A miracle of miniaturized electronics lay inside. The largest components of the radio were the microphone and speaker. Using my fingernail I flipped the unit on, ran the tiny slide to the appropriate frequency setting and began reciting a series of recognition numbers. Only a tiny hissing and popping of static came to me.

Finally, after what seemed an eternity, Hawk's voice sputtered out of the speaker.

"N3, sir," I said. "I've got to make this fast. I've made contact with Kohar and have the information. The Soviets are massing for their attack through the Khyber Pass within a month."

"Any indication of an exact date?"

"None. Kohar either didn't know or wasn't saying. Can the satellite recon pick up the troop movement?"

A hesitation, then, "One of our VELA satellites has some new pictures, N3. It shows concentrations of Russian troops between Kabul and the Khyber Pass. With their tanks, APCs and helicopters, an entire brigade can be through the pass in less than a week."

"Brigade strength?" I said. "Can they risk that many men?"

"They've reinforced. Their troop strength now exceeds one hundred thousand."

"This is it, then."

"I'm afraid so, N3." A long pause. "N3?"

"Yes, sir?"

"Your assignment remains the same. Go into the Khyber Pass region and report back anything of interest both to our department and the Pentagon."

"Any backup, sir?"

"We can't get anyone else into the region in time. You'll be on your own, just as you are now. Nick, this is vital to world security."

"Am I to take any offensive action against the Russians?"

"That's not in your orders. Observe, but . . ."

"Yes, sir?"

"But if the opportunity comes up for you to safely engage in counterinsurgency, you might consider it."

"Without backup."

"You understand the situation perfectly, N3."

The shuffling sounds of slippered feet against travertine marble alerted me to an unannounced visitor.

"N3 out."

"Good luck."

Even before the word "luck" came from the speaker, I had the lining back in the suitcase and readied myself for a fight. My Luger came to hand as I slid down behind the low bed, peering over it.

A woman—without a veil—came into the room. Her skin was darker than the other Moslem women I'd glimpsed darting around the periphery of Kohar's house. While the veil wasn't required inside the *purdah*, the place where the most faithful of Moslems isolated their women, no outsider was allowed in. Still, save for the veil, this woman was dressed in Moslem style. She wore the dark gray *borqa'* which covered her like a billowing tent and totally erased any hint of figure.

Then it hit me. She wasn't Moslem at all. She wore a tiny red dot directly between her eyes. She was Hindu.

"Mister Carter?" came the hesitant voice. "Please, you are in danger."

I rose, the gun still in hand. Her dark eyes widened even more at the sight of the weapon and she took a step back, flattening herself against the marble wall.

"Who are you?"

"I am Ananda Dasai. I . . . I saw you leave Haj's quarters. You killed him, didn't you?"

"Why warn me I'm in trouble?"

"I want you to escape."

"And?"

"Take me with you."

I shook my head in disbelief. The Moslems guard their women as closely as they do their religious beliefs. In some ways, the two are indistinguishable. Family life and the Mohammedan faith are intertwined in complex ways. If I spat upon the Prophet I couldn't achieve a more cutting insult than stealing away one of Kohar's women.

"I . . . I am not of their faith. Achmed keeps me as a slave. I want to return to my own people, though I am shamed."

"Look, Ananda, it's not going to be easy for me to get out of here by myself. Haj," I said, using the name she'd given the dead man, "was a Russian KGB agent. He recognized me and tried to report my presence. I had to stop him."

"You are an American agent." She didn't say it as a question, she knew.

"That's right. And when Kohar finishes his afternoon prayers, finds Haj dead, there'll be hell to pay." I hefted the suitcase and started to push past her. A petite hand, surprisingly strong, gripped at my sleeve and stopped me.

"I must leave. They will kill me. I am Hindu." Her

eyes dropped, then rose to mine. I sighed. My options weren't too satisfactory at the moment. Leaving Ananda behind was out of the question. She'd try to trade her knowledge for her life; Kohar would be on my trail the instant I left this room. I should kill her. She'd already said that Achmed Kohar would do that, anyway.

Call me a sucker. Cold-blooded killing has never been popular with me.

"Okay, come along. You're going to have to tell me the best way out of this place, though. It's like a maze inside."

"This way." Ananda gripped my hand and pulled me along. I cursed having to carry the suitcase, but it contained my transmitter and other equipment which would prove useful. While I didn't need the camera, telephoto lenses, binoculars and other optical equipment inside, it made spying long distance a lot easier.

She pulled me along, through the women's quarters, past where the eunuch was usually positioned, past the gallery where forty people knelt on rugs in prayer to Allah, then to a side door. Parked outside was the immensely long Mercedes limo.

I tossed my bag in the back and slipped behind the wheel. No keys. Hugo flashed into my hand and I dived under the dashboard. It took long minutes to get around the steering wheel lock and hotwire the ignition. The car started with a ragged cough, then turned as smooth as silk. I slammed it into gear and raced off, startling the chickens idly pecking at grain in the courtyard.

I didn't know how long we had so this time couldn't be wasted.

"How do we get north, to Peshawar?"

"Peshawar!" she cried. "That's near my home. You would take one fallen in caste home?"

"I'm going in that direction." My tone cut off any further inquiry in that direction. Ananda Dasai didn't need to know why I wanted to scout along the mountains, peer into the Hindu Kush and start up a brush war against the Soviets.

"I am disgraced because my husband is dead."

"Kohar killed him?"

"That is true. Achmed Kohar is not a man to anger. When my husband tried to prevent Kohar from raising opium poppies on our land, Kohar killed him. His gaze fell upon me and, for whatever reason, he found me desirable. If I had converted to the Moslem faith, I might have even been one of his wives."

"He's got several?"

"Forty. But even if I had wanted to give up my faith, it would never have worked out. His first wife does not like me. She agitated with his other wives to make me an outcast, which, with the death of my husband, is exactly what I am."

"If you depend on your husband's position so much, find some unattached guy and marry him. You're quite pretty." I wasn't just saying that. Ananda had an exotic beauty that would make her very popular in any Western country. While I couldn't tell anything about her figure under the tentlike garment, I bet it was as sensational as her finely boned face, the intelligent dark eyes, the high forehead, the firm chin and slender throat.

She averted her eyes, then looked up at me, saying, "It is more than that. By Hindu faith, I can never remarry. No matter how my husband died. There is no divorce, no remarriage. While I am not an outcast, I do not belong anywhere. We no longer practice *suttee,* the widow's immolation on her husband's funeral pyre, but I sometimes regret that modernization. Life is difficult for me."

"Why go back to your village, then?"

"My brother is a charitable soul. He has much good karma and might take me back, even though he does not have to do so."

"So let's get you back north and see. What's the best way of proceeding?" I checked the gas gauge—almost empty. Even with armed guards and a chauffeur constantly watching the car, pilferage must be great in Pakistan. Kohar probably never kept much fuel in the limousine, except when he took longer trips.

"The train station."

"Lahore?"

"No, just down the road, some ten kilometers. We can catch the shuttle from here to the main line. Mughalpura is the repair depot for the Pakistan Western Railroad."

That was a bit of information I hadn't known. Checking the rear view mirror made it even more important. Dust clouds rose around Kohar's mansion. The drug supplier had either found Haj's body or discovered one of his household gone. It might have been either Ananda or me. Whatever the reason, he'd loosed the hounds.

"Down this fork," she said, pointing. In the distance I saw the railroad spur. Machine shops stood on either side of the tracks and at the head was a large warehouse, a barn for parking out-of-service engines. We rattled over the narrow-gauge tracks—they couldn't have been more than a two and a half feet apart. But that didn't stop the size of the engines from being immense.

One puffed and grunted and chuffed white smoke into the air, readying itself for the trip to Lahore.

"There's our transportation," I said, slamming on the brakes and careening to a halt. "Let's go."

We bailed out and ran, Ananda working to get her veil in place as she did. Hindu women didn't obey the law of the veil, but her disguise required her to blend in. An unveiled woman would be instantly spotted, drawing unwanted attention.

I heaved my suitcase into the single car behind the engine. The car itself was empty, being shuttled back into Lahore after some no doubt major overhaul. Minor repairs went begging in this country, like so many other things.

I felt hot streaks graze my arm and back without hearing the reports. Kohar's men chased us, firing as they came. I pulled hard and got into the car. Ananda stumbled and missed the handgrip, then regained her balance and started running. Reaching down from the car, I grabbed her arm and swung her inside.

"Thank you," she said. I saw tears in her eyes. She'd come close to death. There wasn't any telling what Kohar would have done to her for aiding me.

"Let's just sit back and enjoy the ride into Lahore," I

said. "I doubt if the engineer even knows we're aboard."

Bits of wood flew out of the doorjamb as we entered the car. I ducked, shoving Ananda to one side and going in the other. Crouched behind one of the rickety seats, I drew my Luger. Kohar's men had gotten onto the car at the rear at the last possible instant. They now stalked us.

I wondered if they knew I had a gun, or if it mattered to them. Whatever I did to them had to be less severe than the punishment Kohar dished out for failure. Waiting is the hardest thing in the world, and if you do it successfully great rewards will be yours.

It worked that way with me.

I let the men completely enter the car and begin their way down the aisle. The rocking to and fro threw them off balance as they walked, making aiming difficult. I spun into the aisle, braced my wrist against the edge of the seat and began firing slow, measured rounds. The first two killed a burly man dressed in a Western-style business suit. The third took out the man behind. By this time the third and final man realized what was happening and opened fire.

Bullets flew wildly. I ducked again, waiting for him to calm down. When the last round smashed into the wood over my head, I counted to one hundred, then rolled into the aisle, staying on my belly this time. He'd grown impatient and had started to advance again.

One easy shot to the head removed him.

I got to my feet and checked. All three were dead. I turned to Ananda and saw she sat in a pool of blood. For a split second I thought she'd been hit, but realized it was the blood of the first man I shot.

"It's over," I said, knowing that wasn't true. I threw the bodies out the rear, wondering how many men Achmed Kohar would send after us. The answer kept coming out too high for comfort.

SEVEN

Again I was struck by the incredible difference between the thronging city of Lahore and the affluence of Achmed Kohar. The people in the street bartered chickens and goat cheese and skins and eked out the most minimal of lives while the dope dealer sat fat and happy behind the fifteen-foot walls of his mansion, selling the illicit products of his poppy fields to international dealers in misery and individual destruction. I wished there was some way of stopping Kohar and the others like him, but that wasn't my mission. Not this time.

In a way, my mission was even more complex than stopping drug trafficking. I had to go north to Peshawar, then into the Khyber Pass area, and do what I could to stop the Russian incursion over the border. That wasn't exactly the way Hawk had put it, but his meaning had been clear. I gathered information to send back to the Pentagon and State Department, but I was also the first—and last—line of defense for an entire country.

Without the aid I could give, Pakistan would soon fall to the Russian bear.

The crowd jostled and pressed against us. Bodies tried to pull away the suitcase I carried. It hadn't been the smartest or easiest way of carrying all my equipment, but it had been convenient and Kohar expected to see a visitor to his mansion lugging such baggage. The only plus in the trip from the freight yard in Lahore, where the repaired trains were sided off to more produc-

41

tive routes, was having Ananda along.

While dressed in veil and *borqa'* disguised her and let her blend in with the other women in the Muslim city, it also provided the opportunity for her to speak without being seen. Her soft voice gave me a running account of what happened around me.

The street beggars controlled the crime. They masterminded the pickpockets and cutpurses like Arabic Fagins. The urchins thronging the streets were their bread and butter, darting in, grabbing and running, then turning over the entire proceeds to their masters. A few blind men rattled cans and begged for alms; Ananda told me some were actually blind but that many weren't. For all that deception, I saw enough real deformity and mutilation to sicken me.

"In my country," she said, her voice resigned, "mothers often mutilate their children by cutting off a hand or crushing a foot. Evidence of need inspires the generous and gullible to give a bit more."

"What about them?" I asked, lifting my chin slightly to indicate an odd band at the edge of the railway platform. Some juggled, some begged, others danced to the rhythmic beatings on the bottom of an old coffee can. What struck me as peculiar was their dress. The group was obviously all men, yet they dressed in the *shalwar* and patterned *qamiz* reserved for women.

"They are *hijira*," she said, obvious displeasure in her voice. "I have no word for it other than this."

"Transvestites? Men who dress as women?"

"Yes, that is the *hijira*. They entertain and beg and perform sexual acts with other men." Again the distaste. "They are worse than the Hindu outcastes."

I glanced behind, an uneasy feeling building. In the bustle of the crowd on the platform, it wasn't possible to pick out individuals, yet I did. There was an air of determination about them. Maybe they were better fed, their clothes a little finer than those surrounding us. Whatever it was, I spotted four men working their way through the crowd, sometimes spinning men around and peering closely at them, then releasing their temporary victim and moving on. These four sought someone.

They sought me.

"When's the train for Peshawar?" I asked.

"That must be it coming now." Ananda gestured down the tracks. In the distance, I saw the tall white plumes from the steam engine curling up into the air.

"Where's this train bound for?" I felt a bit foolish having to ask, but my knowledge of the Arabic letters was severely limited. Given time and painful concentration, I could work out the curlicues and squiggles. I didn't have that time now, not with Kohar's men after me.

Or were they Kohar's men? Haj had been a KGB double agent. These might be local KGB agents come to avenge the death of their fellow agent. Whoever they represented made little difference. The difference between a shot between the eyes and a knife through the heart is moot. Dead is dead, no matter who causes it.

"It is for Karachi."

"Onto the train," I said, shoving her ahead of me, not allowing her to protest. I cursed myself for stupidity when I noticed that we had become the center of attention. It wasn't done that way in Pakistan. I hurried ahead of Ananda, letting her stay the proper three paces behind. I jumped onto the train just as it gathered forward momentum. I had to reach out and grab her just as I had in Mughalpura because the flowing *borqa*' prevented easy maneuvering. With Ananda beside me, I motioned for her to speed up. I got inside the car and forced my way to the grimy window and peered out.

The four men had seen us hurriedly climbing on.

"To the back of the car. Damn it, run!" I shouted, pushing her along and trying to keep the suitcase with all my gear inside from knocking out teeth and bruising those already seated.

A bullet smashed into the wall at head level. Ananda dived and got through the connecting door leading to the next car. I slammed the door behind me but instead of going on back, I pulled her aside so that we jumped onto the platform. The train had gained considerable speed and the impact jarred me. For Ananda, it wasn't quite as bad. If the *borqa'* hindered her movement, it also padded the falls.

"Come on. Back to the Peshawar train," I said.

"Wait, please, I am out of breath."

"No time. Hurry it up before they figure out what happened." I wanted the four men on the train bound for Karachi. By the time they'd searched and discovered we weren't aboard, I intended being halfway to Peshawar.

The time it took to get to the spot where the Peshawar train boarded made it necessary for us to again go through our act of me jumping aboard, then pulling Ananda in after me. By now, I had it down pat and so did she. She swung in and smiled.

"You are very strong." Her hand lingered on my arm for a moment. Our gazes locked and communication flowed that was more than words.

"Let's find our cabin."

"Cabin?" she asked, surprised. "That is deluxe travel. I have never traveled any way but third class."

I shuddered at the thought of being in the baggage car. First class was barely tolerable. I remembered the ride in from Islamabad in first class. I'd shared my seat with equal numbers of humans and barnyard animals.

"A cabin," I said firmly. The number of people in Pakistan wealthy enough to afford a compartment didn't travel often to Peshawar up on the northern border. A little dickering with the conductor, a large bribe for him—less than five dollars American—and Ananda and I were in our own minuscule cabin. Twin beds folded down out of the wall and left almost no room at all. Those and a window only slightly cleaner than the others in the car were the only advantages to traveling deluxe class.

"I hope the engine doesn't go off the tracks," I said. The train rolled heavily from side to side on the narrow-gauge road, indicating loose track and overloading of the boxcars. "Why don't they build all the tracks wide enough to match those in other parts of the world?"

"These were originally built by the British to supply their troops. They had no reason to build tracks for commercial shipment. If anything, they wanted to keep the use of precious wood in the ties down to a minimum."

"You're pretty well up on the history, Ananda. I detect a hint of British accent, too."

"I have attended London University," she said. "It is my sorrow I did not complete my courses to a degree."

"Why not?"

"I met Suman, we fell in love, married, returned to Pakistan. My family was outraged. They are traditional in many ways, quite liberal in others. My brother and I are all that remain of fourteen children. Gupta is *chaudry* for our village and had responsibilities that prevented him from going to England. While I am only a woman, I was sent by the combined efforts of my parents, uncles and cousins. I was not to marry; that is a matter for the father to arrange."

"Western ways are to your liking?" I saw the light come to her eyes.

"Oh, yes! Your women are so free, yet . . ."

"Yet what?"

"They do not observe tradition. That is their failing—your culture's failing. There is no bond in families. To my disgrace I have discovered this."

"Why'd you come back to Pakistan?"

"Suman was a civil engineer. He worked on a sewage project in our village and was killed by them."

The way she emphasized the word "them" showed special meaning. I waited, saying nothing, studying her. She had pushed back the cowl on the *borqa'* to reveal the clean, dark lines of her face. She was a pawn caught between two cultures—one old and venerating the status quo and the other worshiping continual change. She'd disobeyed tradition by choosing her own husband instead of allowing the family to pick and barter for her like a sheep or cow. I suspected she'd been accepted back into her village's society, however, because of her husband's needed skills and the effort that had gone into getting even a partial college education for her.

"The opium growers," she continued. "The ones like Kohar across the border, snipe, loot, soften us up to force our people to grow still more of their poppies."

"I know," I said, recognizing the pattern. The Russians used the same techniques, though neither drug dealer nor communist had invented them. The Soviets went for the village leaders, those educated who might oppose them. Kill them, re-educate others in the ways of Lenin and Marx, start a People's Revolution and then the fuse was lit.

A knock sounded on the door. Due to our cramped position in the room, Ananda was closer and the obvious one to answer it. Before I could yell a warning, I saw a knife lift and descend through the few inches of space when she'd pulled open the door. She gasped, stumbled, hit her head against the wall and sank to the floor.

The woman's limp body blocked the door. The man in the hall had to kick twice to shove her body out of the way. By this time I was ready for him. In a flash I'd considered using Wilhelmina but decided against it. While the train moving over the narrow tracks was noisy, I didn't want to risk having a dozen curious faces looking in to see where the gunshot came from.

My stiletto leaped into hand.

The man was one of the four I'd seen on the Lahore train platform. Either he hadn't gotten on the Karachi-bound train or he'd been able to get off in time to follow us. While I couldn't be one hundred percent sure, I thought that removing him eliminated all danger to us. The other three men simply didn't have the quickness to come after us. I'd have seen them from the platform if they had.

He stabbed out. Hugo turned aside the thrust and winged inward. The tip found flesh. The man let out a howl of rage and pain, kicked at Ananda's body on the floor and stumbled. The tightness of the compartment kept him from moving as he'd have liked. He thrashed around like a bull with its tail in a meat grinder, trying to keep his balance. That was fine with me. While the woman's limp form occupied his feet, I kept his knife hand busy parrying thrust after thrust.

He was good, but the would-be assassin hesitated once. That was his downfall. My stiletto slashed out across his throat. Eyes widening in shock, he dropped his knife and clutched at the spurting well under his chin. I jerked up the window, grabbed a handful of cotton shirt and heaved. The motion of the train aided me. The dying man catapulted out the window, to lie jerking beside the tracks.

After closing the window, I sheathed Hugo, slammed the door and bent over Ananda.

"My arm," she said. "It is numb."

I had to laugh. The vicious looking knife blow hadn't even scratched her. The blade had tangled her unwieldy *borqa'* and the force had knocked her to the floor. Hitting her head against the wall, she had lain unconscious on her arm until the circulation had left it. Other than this she was in fine shape.

Just how fine I couldn't help but notice. The knife had sliced through the heavy cloth. Ananda wore nothing under it.

She saw where I looked.

"They did not allow me anything else. Why waste valuable clothing on a slave?"

"Why, indeed," I said. I bent forward and kissed her. Somehow the movement of the train rocking back and forth no longer seemed out of place. If anything, it added an air of sexiness. My hands worked through thick folds and lifted the garment from her. In the light filtering through the window she sat like a perfectly formed mahogany figurine: small, petite, delightful to touch.

She reached out and took my hands, pulling them toward her apple-sized breasts. I kissed her again, even as she began stripping off my unwanted clothing.

I pulled her down on one of the beds. We both tumbled into it, not caring at all about the smallness. My hands roamed her slim body, following the sleek lines, finding delicious valleys. Hers concentrated on one area of mine. I responded immediately to her touch.

"It has been a long while," she said. "Since my husband."

"Kohar didn't . . . ?"

"What? With a Hindu? Never. He might sacrifice his place in paradise with the faithful *houris* if he dared violate me. I scrubbed and cleaned, did the menial tasks."

I silenced her with another kiss. Again the rocking of the train aided rather than hindered our movements. We moved with the rhythmic motion, her legs parting for me. I slipped within her, felt her dampness and warmth, then let the swaying train carry our locked bodies to a paradise of our own creation.

Afterward we slept, arms and legs entwined. It wasn't until the train whistle hooted raucously to indicate that we were nearing Peshawar that we stirred and eventually dressed.

EIGHT

I walked along the train platform, suitcase in my left hand and my right resting lightly on the holstered Luger. While I was virtually sure that the single assassin on the train hadn't had time to pass along where we were and where we headed, I couldn't be absolutely sure.

My caution proved unneeded. We left the train station and went toward Peshawar, a city even more poverty-stricken than Lahore. No taxis ran from the depot to the city proper, so we walked. I was acutely conscious of Ananda's hip lightly brushing against mine as we trudged along. My thoughts kept returning to the fact that she wore nothing under her tentlike *borqa'*.

"My village is less than fifteen kilometers from the Khyber Pass, to the southeast" she said. "It is rather isolated and small. It is why a small group of Hindus can live peacefully in this Moslem country. The Russian guerrillas come through occasionally, since the pass is not as heavily guarded as when the British held this area."

I remembered vividly the relief map I'd studied back in Washington. The Khyber Pass was important because it was about the only way across the mountains in this vicinity without outfitting a complete rock-climbing team.

I'm in good shape, and yet I found my lungs straining just a bit to keep up with her ground-devouring pace. As much as I hated to admit it, I've gotten used to the Western way of driving wherever I go, even if it's just around the block. In this part of the world autos of any kind were scarce and even more scarce was the gasoline to run them.

"Do we walk all the way to your brother's house?" I finally asked.

"No," she said, smiling. "You have much money. Let's ask this caravan master if we can ride."

She indicated a man leading a string of moth-eaten camels. I sighed. I've ridden camels before and found it wearing both on the body and the nerves. Their peculiar rolling gait makes travel difficult, although some of the more experienced actually sleep while atop the bad-tempered beasts. Even as we approached, one of them chundered at me. The thick, vile gob just missed me; I moved fast enough to avoid it. The beast turned a half-lidded eye on me, as if the miss were something to be avenged later.

Ananda argued, bartered and finally got us berths aboard a pair of the camels.

In spite of the short distance, it took two days to reach Ananda's village nestled on the side of a mountain tall enough to intimidate most of its lesser cousins in the United States. I paid an outrageous sum to the caravan master for allowing us the use of his camels and then watched the man continue on.

"What's in his cargo?" I asked Ananda. "Not farm goods."

She laughed. "He is an Afridi," she said, as if that said everything. Seeing I didn't understand, she added, "All Afridis are gun runners. It is a cottage industry with them. They sell the guns to all throughout the Khyber Pass region. We do not receive foreign aid so we must help ourselves. Really, the Afridis are capable gunsmiths."

I made a mental note of that. Hawk might find it interesting that a local industry had built up around gun manufacture and supply.

"I . . . I do not know if I should even bother returning to my brother's house." Ananda dropped her eyes and stood silently.

"It wasn't your fault Suman was killed by the drug dealers. It certainly wasn't your fault you ended up in Kohar's household as a slave."

"I am without a husband," she said in a low voice. "I am not an outcast, but I am near."

"You said your brother was a progressive sort. Let's find out. If Gupta Dasai is as smart as you credit him with being, he'll take you in." The nuances of Hindu society eluded me, but from her comments about unity of family and strength of community, it hardly seemed likely her only remaining brother would cast her out. Still, I didn't know that for sure. She might become more of a burden to me than a help if Gupta Dasai didn't allow her to stay. Ananda promised to give me a stable base of operation—from here all the way into the Khyber Pass, and maybe beyond—if her brother took her back.

As we walked in silence, I felt eyes on us from all quarters. I ignored that as much as I could in favor of sizing up their defenses. What I saw didn't please me too much. There hadn't been any rhyme or reason to the way the village had been laid out. Even the most elementary of plans hadn't been followed. Sanitation was badly needed, the streets were filthy with cows and cow dung and worst of all, from a military standpoint, the village was totally undefensible.

The mountain on one flank should have been a plus factor. These people had turned it into a liability. A few soldiers with machine guns or mortars could command the entire area from those foothills. With any luck, a few pounds of high explosives might even bring down an avalanche and save them the price of bullets. The other approaches to the village were even worse—from the point of view of a resident.

A dirt path angled off downslope toward the valley leading to the Khyber Pass. A single tank could charge up that barren valley with little to stop it. In the direction we'd come it was even worse. Open spaces on either side of the road afforded poor farmland, about the only flat area to be seen. Entire armies could march through it unscathed. The best hope for anyone in this village under attack would be to either run or surrender, and hope their conqueror was merciful.

I doubted the Russians would slaughter them outright, as they'd done so many times in Afghanistan. The Soviet's chief purpose wasn't to hold this land as much as use it as a pathway for a blitzkrieg through Pakistan down to Karachi and into India. According to our intelligence reports, that's the way the Russian Army has been trained. Quick, decisive action with troops, tanks and gunships. They aren't geared for a long, drawn out, grinding war of attrition, such as the Mujeheddin in Afghanistan have engaged in.

While the raw material here didn't look too promising, perhaps something in the way of a militia could be formed to slow down the Russian advance and make them take notice. If so, that'd give our diplomats time to convince the Indian government that the Soviets weren't the friends and allies they'd thought.

To win that time, this village might have to be sacrificed.

"This is my brother's house," Ananda said, stopping. The political leader of more than five hundred people lived little better than those he served. The house might have been larger than most I'd seen, but it was a fractional difference. The walls were a combination of wood and mud bricks and the roof sported red baked-clay tiles.

"How many live in the house?" I asked.

"My brother Gupta, his wife, their four children, his wife's uncles, Nandin and Hara, and my parents." Ananda said this last with deep regret. She had to face them with the news that she had become disgraced due to her husband's death. They'd no doubt pass this off as karma, for her marrying without their permission.

"Is Gupta the real head of the family, or is your father?"

"My father is *malik*, the head of our lineage, but Gupta is the village *chaudry*. He alone is responsible for the well-being of those living here. He does a good job, and my father does not often interfere with Gupta's decisions."

"Let's do some fancy talking," I said. We went to the door and knocked. A slender man answered. His face remained impassive, but his eyes took on a glow when he saw Ananda.

"Sister," he said softly.

"Brother."

"Your husband is dead," Gupta told her. "I am sorry. It is karma. But he was a good man and lived a good life, helping make lives safer in our country. He will soon be reincarnated."

"In a better form," she said. Turning, Ananda announced, "This man is Nick Carter, an American. He has aided me in my disgrace."

I bristled at her phrasing, but let it pass since Gupta Dasai nodded knowingly.

"Thank you, Mister Carter, for my village and my family."

"What?" demanded Ananda. "For the family?"

"Yes, little sister, our parents are dead. Last week the guerrillas again came. They killed them when our father resisted their attempts to steal our food. Crops have not been good."

"How many guerrillas were there?" I asked.

"Enough. The Shinwari tribesmen no longer have complete control over travel through the Khyber Pass. The Russians leak through like some pestilence." Dasai's voice turned even more bitter. "I am now head of the Dasai family."

"Brother—"

"There is no need to ask, little sister. My beliefs are not as rigid as those of our parents. Still, my position is not the strongest. I will take you into the house, but my wife's uncles will treat you as a pariah, an outcast."

"Thank you, Gupta."

"Has there been any more guerrilla activity?" I asked, now that the family problems were at least partially solved. "Did your parents die as the guerrillas went into Pakistan or as the guerrillas were returning?"

"They have not penetrated far. This is still Pakistan, though the distinction in these mountains is small. We chased the Russian lackeys back into Afghanistan. Let the Mujeheddin have them."

"You can't defend the village very well," I pointed out. "These raids are going to become more frequent. Do you have a militia, some sort of civil defense? An incendiary bomb could send a fire raging through these houses. Is there ample water to fight the fires?"

"You speak as a soldier." It wasn't accusation as much as simple statement of fact.

"I desire your continued safety here."

"Life is but an illusion. *Maya*. Your concern is touching." Gupta's tone indicated he thought otherwise. I was an outsider meddling where I didn't belong, and he wanted to tell me but not in front of Ananda. This wasn't women's talk.

"My concern is further reaching than your village. I'd like to give you some training in how to stop the Russian guerrillas before they pour through the pass and inundate all of Pakistan. They will not stop with simple occupation. Your religion will be banned."

"This is the strength of Hinduism," Gupta said. "It is not organized, it has no creed or dogma. We absorb from those around us; we do not convert. Hinduism is a catalogue of rituals and duties, primarily duties to one's self and family. It brings order to our person and allows us to achieve personal, inner progress."

"The Russians will prevent any personal progress with a bullet in your heart," I said.

Gupta shrugged, as if saying, "So what? It is karma."

"I know quite a bit about their tactics. I can aid you in designing defenses."

"Defenses?" He laughed harshly. "The Muhmand are warriors second to none. We *fight*. We need no defenses to cower behind."

That sounded like a suicidal philosophy to me, but I remained silent. With Ananda, I went into the house to meet the rest of the family. None of them even spoke to us.

Defending this village looked like a more difficult task all the time. If I hadn't needed it as a base, I would have moved on and to hell with them.

NINE

Flopped on my belly in the thin, stony dirt, I braced the binoculars and slowly panned the countryside. What I saw I didn't like one bit. The furtive movement of men through the choppy terrain meant only one thing: Soviet infiltration. The Shinwari had let more of the Russian guerrillas through the Khyber Pass past Fort Jamrud. In the old days, when the sun never set on the British Empire, Fort Jamrud had been immense, imposing. The pictures I'd seen of it showed the battlements bristling with machine guns, a veritable Rock of Gibraltar in the middle of the highest mountains on earth. But now, without ever having seen the fort firsthand, I knew it no longer proved as effective.

It couldn't and let so many guerrillas through.

I figured at least fifty armed men worked their way toward Gupta Dasai's village. Putting down the binoculars, I took out the special camera and telephoto lens. This camera electronically recorded the images, giving a resolution even ASA 600 black and white film couldn't match. I took my pictures, showing their movement techniques, getting a couple good shots of their armament—AK-47s, of course—and even of their non-descript clothing. There was no question, however, that these were Soviet troops in mufti.

They didn't look Pathan like Achmed Kohar and his men. They certainly didn't belong on this terrain with their flat faces and sallow complexions. I had them pegged as Mongolian. The Russians kept their eastern province troops in Afghanistan, more as cannon fodder than anything else. As much as the Soviets wanted their warm water port, they weren't so obsessed that they didn't keep their Asiatic "republics" drained of any potential troublemakers by drafting them into the army.

I packed my camera and hurried down the hill. Less than an hour remained before they hit the village.

"Gupta!" I cried out, entering the village. "Russians on the way. About fifty."

"I know."

"How? The trader who came through here earlier—he warned you?"

An itinerate wheeler-dealer had rolled through, his wagon drawn by two of the tiredest-looking oxen I'd ever seen. He'd come from the Khyber Pass area and had spotted the guerrillas. That had to be the answer.

"Yes, the *powindeh* told us. The guerrillas bypassed the Sikh village in favor of striking here again. They fear upsetting the Sikhs."

That made perfect sense to me. The Sikhs were ferocious fighters when roused, as the British had found out during the Sepoy Revolution in 1857. Peaceful for the most part, the Sikhs fought to the last man if they felt their religion was being threatened. The guerrillas didn't want to stir up trouble; they wanted to gain a foothold for the final step down into India. As long as the Sikhs weren't bothered, they wouldn't fight. Dasai's village provided a more vulnerable target for the Russians, especially with such a small guerrilla force.

"What are you going to do about it?" I demanded. "An hour, no longer, before they get here."

Dasai laughed until tears rolled down his face.

"I am sorry, Carter. You do not understand. The Sikhs are mighty warriors. So are the Muhmand." He gestured around him, indicating his village. "We will never allow ourselves to be subjugated. We have Afridi-made weapons." He reached behind a low shed and pulled out a rifle newly made but old in design. It looked like a 1925 Martini-Henry lever action. Dasai proudly displayed it for my approval.

I took it, levered out a shell and examined the workings.

"Why not steal something newer to copy?" I asked. "Their assault rifles—the AK-47s—are simple to duplicate."

"Many have the British Lee-Enfield," Dasai declared.

I sighed. This was hardly more modern.

"Why not something like a Bren gun? Or a Sten gun? Those are real cottage industry weapons. Even an Uzi."

"These are unknown to me. This is known." He took the Martini-Henry and fondly patted it. "And we will show you there is nothing to fear. We Muhmand can defend ourselves."

"Be with you in a few minutes," I told Dasai. "Got to make sure all my gear is put away before the fight." I went into his house, past the main entry and the room off it, back to the *hujra,* the guest quarters. Unpacking my camera, I slipped out the ceramic block holding my pictures, then opened the suitcase. Stripping out the lining revealed a small cavity just large enough to accommodate the picture block. I dropped it in, checked the settings, then turned on the transmitter. It took several minutes for me to reach Hawk.

"Go ahead, N3, report," came his brusque voice. I imagined I even smelled his cigar and saw him shift it from one side of his mouth to the other impatiently waiting for me to continue.

"Yes, sir," I said. "Transmitting pictures, three, two, one, now."

"Got them," he said. "Hmm, nice shots of the Soviet guerrillas. Where were these taken?"

"A mile from here. This is the calm before the storm."

"I see."

I told him what little I'd discovered, touching lightly on Achmed Kohar, the certainty that Haj had been a KGB agent and my displeasure over the quality of arms in Gupta Dasai's village.

"There is little we can do about that, N3," he said. "The CIA wants to begin some covert activity but cannot. Usual snafu on their part. They have a news leak in their department, and one of the Washington columnists got hold of the details. They're having to lie low for a while. You're on your own, N3."

"No way you could get me an air strike in the next few minutes?" I asked facetiously. Hawk didn't bother answering.

"Keep me posted. The Pentagon is interested, and the State Department is foaming at their collective mouths over this. The pictures will do much to convince the powers that be in New Delhi that Soviet adventurism is on the rise and aimed at them."

"Right, sir. Will report later."

"Good work, N3."

Static claimed the channel. I replaced the ceramic block in my camera, pressed the erase button and had a good-as-new "film" magazine in it again. The radio and other components put back into their case, I lugged the entire mess out and carried it some distance from the house. No place would be safe after the guerrillas overran the village—I saw no other possible outcome—so I wanted my equipment out of the way.

After the task of hiding the case had been finished, I went back to the front of Dasai's house. He had finished oiling his rifle and proudly ran round after round through the chamber.

"Would you like to see how it handles?" he asked.

"If you've got a spare one, I'll try it out—on a guerrilla."

He laughed, his even white teeth flashing in the late sun. The time of day was about all we had in our favor. The Soviet troops had to move into the setting sun. We had the slight chance of spotting them from reflections off their equipment. It didn't seem like much of an edge.

"You worry too much, Carter. We are fighters. These cow eaters will not take our village."

"You've lost your parents; Ananda's lost her husband. You're not doing such a good job so far."

The smile left Dasai's face.

"We fight. Take this." He shoved the rifle into my hands. I tested it for balance and had to admit it felt good. The real test was yet to come, however. Any rifle can feel right; it takes special talent to make one that shoots accurately at three hundred yards.

From its hiding place Dasai picked up another rifle. Together we silently mounted the same hill from which I'd spotted the guerrillas. We dropped down, Dasai putting a single box of shells between us.

"Twenty shells?" I asked. "Don't expect much of a fight, do you?"

"It will be sufficient," he said.

I didn't share his confidence. I studied the terrain once more and didn't like the way it looked for our side. If the guerrillas took the hill Dasai and I guarded, the way into the village was open. I doubted two of us, even with modern weapons, could hold back a force of fifty guerrillas for long.

"There," he said suddenly. "They come."

I hefted the rifle, sighted and slowly squeezed off a round. It went too far up and to the right. Dasai's rifle barked almost at the same instant. He dropped his man. I adjusted my sights and tried again. Another miss.

"We can't keep this up," I told Dasai. "They know we're here. They can even rush us and take the hill."

"Good. Let them rush us. We will retreat."

"It's either that or be slaughtered," I said, firing again. I think I wounded my target, but at the distance we fought it was impossible to tell. Then I didn't worry about firing. A fusillade of heavy slugs ripped into the hillside. They'd opened up with a machine gun.

"Let them use their ammo," Dasai said confidently. After a few minutes, he rolled back into position and began firing in a slow, measured sequence. I joined him. This time I saw two guerrillas go down under my fire. But our ammunition was down to five shells between us.

Four shells, two, then one. We both reached for it at the same time. Dasai bowed ironically and gave me the solitary bullet. I wounded a man trying to sneak up the hill. I slung the rifle around my back and pulled out my Luger.

"No," said Dasai. "Not that. Come. Retreat."

I reluctantly abandoned my position. If he'd brought another few boxes of ammunition, we could have picked off at least five more guerrillas before having to turn tail and run. Still, I was glad to be leaving. The heat of battle had caused me to breathe faster than normal. The high altitude robbed me of wind. When we began dog-trotting down the hill heading toward the village, I was almost gasping for air.

"Not here," he said, strong fingers locking like steel bands on my arm. "Up there."

Then I understood his tactics. In these mountains, there is always a hill higher than the one you're on. The hill from which we'd sniped was a decent climb, yes, but one nearer the village provided an even better vantage point. We huffed and puffed and ran all the way up. Five others already atop this hill had their rifles in gun rests. Several hundred rounds of ammunition littered the small area. I dropped down and took my place.

We didn't have long to wait.

The guerrillas charged over the hill we had just abandoned, thinking they'd met all the resistance there was. The devastating fire from this mountain cut them down like rows of wheat before a scythe. In the distance I heard new rifles opening up.

"From the flanks. They tried to go down the sides of that hill. The others take care of them. The only path of retreat is back the way they come."

"Never corner a rat, eh?" I said. I'd have preferred to eliminate all the guerrillas rather than allow any to escape and report back, but this was Dasai's show. He'd done much better than I'd given him credit for. Still, this wasn't more than a skirmish. If the Russians were serious about taking this village, they wouldn't use guerrilla troops next time. They'd risk some air support.

"See? They run like whipped dogs! Come, back down and after them!"

"What?" I cried. "No, don't. Wait!"

But Dasai and the others left this mountain and re-turned to the lower hill to continue firing at the re-treating Soviet guerrillas.

I stayed on high ground and watched. Of the fifty guerrillas, at least half escaped. Not too bad for a bunch of hill people, but they didn't know what they'd un-leashed. The next assault wouldn't be this easily turned back. I slung my rifle and wearily headed down into the village. I had to talk with Ananda and see if she couldn't convince her brother to do more in the way of defense before it was too late.

TEN

"They'll make hamburger out of everyone in this village," I said, trying to keep my anger in check. "Look, Ananda, I know how the Russians operate. They want this position for strategic purposes. They're not going to stop until they have it."

"My brother is capable of defending us. He is *chaudry*. He is in command."

"I applaud your loyalty to him. I understand. After all, he did take you back into his house." That had required great bravery on Gupta Dasai's part. His entire family had opposed him, but he was not only *chaudry* for the village, he was now *malik* for the Dasai family. As the leader of the family, he made the decisions. His wife's uncles counseled against Ananda, but Gupta Dasai wouldn't hear them.

"That has nothing to do with my feelings in this matter. Gupta is skilled in mountain warfare. You are not. That is obvious," she said, her dark eyes flashing with a hint of anger. "You did not understand the trap he sprung this afternoon any more than the guerrillas did—until it was too late."

"That was this afternoon. I'm worried about tonight and tomorrow and all the tomorrows after that. The Russians won't give up easily. If they're risking sending guerrilla units across the border, that means they will also try for a helicopter gunship. There have to be machine guns posted on the hills to knock it down when it comes in."

"I won't intervene," Ananda said forcefully. "Besides, if Gupta cannot handle it, Kali can."

"What?" I was stunned. Ananda presented a mixture of the old ways and the new, the enlightened with the superstitious, but I hadn't expected to hear her mouthing invocations to the goddess Kali.

"It is nothing. I did not mean it." But she did. She'd been absolutely serious when she'd said that the goddess Kali would provide relief for them if the villagers faltered.

"Ah, Carter," Dasai called out, coming in with an armload of Russian assault rifles. "Look at my trophies! Do you like them?" He dropped them in a noisy bundle on the floor and began playing with them, loading and unloading, sighting, dry firing.

"Gupta, this is nice. A good idea taking the weapons from those who'd dropped them, but more serious matters have to be discussed."

"For a hedonist American, you worry more than anyone I have ever known. You should relax, meditate. Lose yourself in prayer and touch the higher being within your soul. Even," he said, his voice lowering to a conspiratorial whisper, "enjoy your hedonism."

"We don't need metaphysics as much as we do firepower aimed at the sky. The Soviets will use a helicopter gunship next time. It's part of their tactical scheme. They can't sustain a battle in the field. They strike quickly, either winning or retreating."

"They retreated," Dasai said proudly.

"After they retreat, they retrench and call in air support. They don't have any tanks on the ground or that would be tossed against you. So, it's got to be air."

"We can handle it," the man said negligently, flopping into a woven wicker chair as he began disassembling one of the captured rifles to see how it worked.

"You can't. They use 20mm cannon, rockets, maybe even napalm or poison gas. Ever hear of 'yellow air'? The sky turns yellow after the Russians use their chemical weapons. It's happened throughout all of Southeast Asia. Death is pretty ugly."

"Life is illusion," said Dasai. *"Maya."*

I snorted in disgust. Talking to him was like arguing with a blank wall. My mind checked off all the possible things I might try to save Dasai and his village. The man wandered off to tend to some chores, as uncaring about his impending doom as one of the cattle idly munching a dry clump of grass beside the dirt road. I sat on a rock and tried to think this through. There had to be something one man—me—could do. After all, I had been sent in here as an expert.

"Nick?" came Ananda's soft voice. "Why are you so worried? The Muhmand tribe is one of fierce warriors. We have held back many of the others. The Mahsuds, Yusufzai, and Wazirs all fear us."

"The Russians don't," I said. "You stand between them and their goal. Do you have any idea how powerful Russia is?"

She only shrugged, as if it meant nothing to her.

"They have the world's largest reserves of gold. Last year alone they sold off three hundred tons to buy food. That makes them rich. Their standing army is funded by one of the highest budgets of any country in the world— maybe the highest compared to their gross national product. And they want Karachi for a warm water ocean port."

"I do not understand. They will come here and die for a shipping port?"

"They will. They moved through Finland trying for one and got booted out of the League of Nations because of it. They seized Latvia, Lithuania and Estonia trying for a port. They'll do anything, no matter the cost. That's one reason they went into Afghanistan."

"The Mujeheddin hold them back," she said firmly, not wanting to believe my dire predictions.

"They're a ragtag band of guerrillas, living a subsistence life. Eventually the Russians will wear them down."

"The British never did."

"The Mujeheddin are Moslems. Do you Hindus value their fighting skills so highly?" I hoped to anger her by knocking her religion. It didn't work.

"They seek their own path through the world. Because it is not ours is no reason to think less of their fighting ability." Ananda studied me as if I were an alien from another planet. "Why do you care so much about this village, its people?"

"I value life."

"Life is nothing. It is a pathway through to a better existence, nothing more. If we die, we have a chance for another, better one until we finally get off the *mandala*."

I didn't want to debate theology with her. I wanted to protect her village. "Listen, Ananda, you've seen the West. You know I'm not lying when I tell you that I sincerely think the Russians will be back, this night if they can, with a helicopter gunship. There is no way to defend this village if the helicopter comes."

"My brother is not worried."

"Your brother's a damned fool!" I blurted. I sank back to my rock and shook my head. "Sorry. That's what I think. I've had enough training to know how the Soviets work. They'll come and this place is defenseless against them."

The words hadn't even gotten out of my mouth when I heard the thump-thump-thump of chopper blades. The cold night air carried sounds a long way, and the valley channeled the noise directly into the village. From the sound I couldn't tell the size of the helicopter, but that hardly mattered. They weren't ferrying troops. They'd come in low, machine gunning everything in sight. If there was the slightest hint of resistance that way, the commander might order a drop of their poison gas. The mycotoxin used was particularly nasty, causing a loss of control in the nervous system, a spastic flopping around, then death about an hour later—if you were lucky. If not, the condition remained permanent while life dragged on.

"The Russians?" Ananda asked, her eyes widening.

"Who else? Get your brother. Have him order everyone into the hills. There's no point sticking around here any longer and getting killed."

I grabbed the rifle I'd used and slid a bullet into the chamber. The snick of the bolt closing made me feel a little better, but not much. There had been time. I should have found a way of rousing the villagers, of getting them into position. They might not have been able to fight off the chopper but they could at least have given it a hot time.

The dark form of the helicopter gunship came into view, a giant inky cloud of death in the night. I fired, heard the *ping!* of my slug ricocheting off metal. I began firing slowly, most of the rounds hitting the chopper. It did no real damage, but it might keep them at a slightly higher altitude and give the villagers time to flee.

The noisy barrage from all over the village told me they weren't running.

"Dasai," I cried, "get these people out of here. They're dead if you don't get them under cover."

"This is easy. The Russian ship hangs like a stone in the air. We will shoot it down."

All hell broke loose. Long tongues of flame blasted off either side of the helicopter. The rockets burned grooves in the earth as they sped along before exploding and flattening half the buildings. Then the Soviets really opened up. Their 20mm cannon began firing. I was close enough to see the drums turning, each barrel taking its turn in sending out one of the heavy slugs before turning away and allowing another the same privilege. Even rotating, the guns began smoking from the friction of lead against steel barrel.

I watched in helpless horror as the gunship ripped apart buildings, cattle, people. It didn't matter to the crew. They might not even have a good view of the landscape. The dense shadows due to the lack of artificial lighting in the village hid the worst of the carnage. Only when the helicopter raced off did I poke my head back up.

Less than ten feet away Dasai lay, clutching his side. I hurried to him, but Ananda got there first.

"Take it easy," I said, pulling his hands away from the

bloody wound. It looked worse than it actually was. One of the bullets from the cannon had nicked him. Possibly he had a broken rib from the impact but other damage from the bullet was superficial.

"They—they destroyed all I have. I saw my wife's two uncles cut down. They exploded as the bullets hit them. They *exploded*!" Gupta Dasai had gone into shock. His face had turned almost pasty white, in spite of the normal mahogany complexion, and his hands were icy.

"Get him covered up. I'll check out the rest of the village," I told Ananda. She began tearing off Dasai's shirt to bind the wound.

It took less than fifteen minutes to make the grand tour. Not more than a matchstick stood. Fires burned quietly, set by the rockets. Everywhere the ground was pock-marked from the impact of heavy slugs. Worst of all, from my standpoint, was the ruin left of my suitcase. Several rounds had smashed through it, blowing the contents apart. The binoculars survived, but the photo equipment was gone.

The fused, smoking remains of the radio I held in my hand, then dropped it. No amount of repair helped total destruction.

Returning to Dasai, I said, "How are you?"

"He's in shock, Nick," answered Ananda. "He hears, I think, but his mind isn't working right."

A hand clutched feverishly at my sleeve. Gupta Dasai pulled me down and whispered harshly, "They shall pay for this. They shall pay!"

"Sure, they will," I said, trying to soothe him.

"The Old Man of the Mountains!" he cried. "The Old Man of the Mountains will help us. Kali be praised!"

I felt a chill race up my spine. I knew Dasai was in shock, but this threat sounded more like a promise, like he wasn't out of it.

But that was ridiculous. I began making my own plans for retaliation.

It was time for Nick Carter, Killmaster for AXE, to go to work.

ELEVEN

We camped in the mountains and watched as the Russian guerrillas re-entered the village the next day. They killed one or two who had managed to survive and whom I had missed in my quick tour. Gupta Dasai and Ananda watched beside me. The man's shock had faded, and he seemed more resigned than angry now.

"It is karma," he said. "There is nothing we can do."

"There's plenty we can do," I told him, trying to hold back my anger. "First of all, you're going to learn to fight. You're going to learn how the Russians fight and what to do against them. They've got men and arms, but they're not supermen."

"Our karma is against us. This would have happened no matter how prepared we were."

"That's defeatist thinking," I shouted, my anger getting the better of me. "Dammit, man, they destroyed your village, killed your friends and family, and you intend to sit and meditate?"

"We can do nothing alone."

"I'll show you what can be done," I said earnestly. "We can't destroy all of them, but we can slow them down, make them worry."

"No. This is karma."

"Ananda?" I asked. She shook her head. It wasn't women's work to go looking for vengeance.

"Doesn't your honor mean anything to you? They've insulted you by this massacre."

"Honor means nothing. This is karma. I do not even see the proper *dharma* in this—the moral obligation to retaliation. Our code of honor is not yours."

"I'm going after them, regardless of what you feel." My declaration meant nothing to either of them. They'd decided the matter was closed. Period. I couldn't shame, coerce, or frighten them. Religion is a powerful tool for good, but it can also be a monumental stumbling block to survival.

"What are you going to do, Nick?" Ananda asked.

"Without your help, I've got to be a one-man army. There's no way I can stop that many trained guerrillas, so I have to find some allies who will help."

"You will find none in these mountains," Dasai said positively. At the moment, I had to agree with him. The cultural barriers kept me from truly understanding them and finding the right key. In a Western country, I'd have known right away what to do, what to say and how best to proceed. Now all I had were a few hunches.

"Not willing," I said, "but I can get them to help. I'm sure of it. Please, Gupta, come along. Show me these mountains. You've lived here all your life. Help me find my way. You won't have to do anything. Just be my guide."

"Karma decrees that nothing can be done."

"Be my guide," I implored. Looking to Ananda for help, I saw her wavering. She might believe in the inevitability of events, of her own deeds being rewarded or punished, but she was also caught in a cultural crossfire. She had tasted European society and mores. In that culture, she could be much freer than in her own, especially after her husband had been killed. But Ananda's Hindu upbringing still held her, at least partially.

"Gupta," she said, her voice low. "To guide him is such a small thing."

"Karma," Dasai said, but I felt the cracks beginning to show in his exterior. He slumped, put his head into cupped hands and simply sat for long minutes. None of us said anything. Finally, Dasai looked up, a haunted air about him. "I will do it."

"Good," I said quietly. "I need to know where the nearest Sikh village is."

Gupta Dasai's expression changed to curiosity. He had no idea what I intended to do in a Sikh village. For that matter, neither did I, but I didn't mention that. It would have to be played by ear when we got there.

"This is as close as we dare go unannounced," Dasai said. Ananda dropped down beside me. I was acutely aware of her warmth, her nearness. Pushing such thoughts from my mind, I peered through my binoculars into the village. While at first glance it appeared no different from Dasai's destroyed one, subtle differences emerged as I studied it. The layout was better for defense. They'd posted armed guards at critical spots around the perimeter. In case of air attack, no fewer than four elevated posts served as defensive bunkers. All in all, they'd done a good job with little more than Dasai had had.

"Enough. I've got to go hunting for some of the Russian guerrillas. I'll be back in a while."

"Nick, what are you trying to do?" Ananda asked.

"Stir up some trouble. I'm hoping the Russians aren't more than a few miles away."

"If they stay in this valley, their encampment is only a few kilometers in that direction," Dasai said, pointing.

It was about where I'd decided the guerrillas would be. After their first ground attack had been beaten back, they had to find a spot to recoup, retrench and prepare for further fighting. With the air strike taking out the village, it wouldn't be until morning that the guerrillas would move to completely occupy the town they'd destroyed.

I didn't have much time to convince the Sikhs that they wanted to stop the Russians.

Silent as a ghost, I slipped into the cold night. The thin air sucked away my breath and sapped my strength, then aided me in staying awake when real pain set in from near-frostbite. It had been a long, tiring day and none of us had gotten any sleep. I'd insisted on continuing, in spite of this. Time worked against me. The Russians had chosen this moment to make their preliminary incursion into Pakistan. Stop it now and their major forces would be held back long enough for Hawk to get all the facts before the diplomats in the State Department, so they could convince the Pakistani government in Islamabad and the Indian government in New Delhi.

Time. It was always the crush of time.

Five kilometers outside the perimeter of the Sikh town I found the first evidence of the guerrillas. Empty shell casings littered the road. I gathered some up and put them in my pocket, keeping them from clinking together. Creeping off, I made my way parallel to the road, wary of the deep shadows and the smallest of sounds. My alertness paid off. I heard snoring.

Advancing slowly, I found the sentry taking a nap in the forked limbs of a tree. His AK-47 dangled from a shoulder strap, while his arms and legs circled a sturdy branch. It was almost a shame to disturb him. Almost.

I yanked hard on the man's rifle. The strap tightened around his shoulder and neck. He grabbed for it, thinking it was falling. Instead, he lost his grip and fell heavily to the ground. One quick thrust with Hugo took the careless sentry out permanently.

Taking the gun and all the man's ammunition, I then went closer to the guerrilla camp. Their perimeter security was lax; they felt they'd eliminated the major opposition in the area. The Sikhs wouldn't bother them without reason, and these Russian soldiers intended to bypass the fierce fighters. The Sikhs were Hindus, but with a good mixture of Moslem tossed in. They traced their ascetic religion back to Nanak in the fifteenth century and did not believe in polytheism, castes or smoking tobacco. Maybe it was the latter that made them such able fighters. I longed to take out one of my gold-tipped monogrammed cigarettes and have a smoke, but I still had a few items to collect before I could relax.

I sidled along just outside the patrol area and found their supply dump. Two men guarded it. I stood, slung the rifle over my shoulder and boldly walked over to them.

"I'm here to relieve you," I said in Russian.

"So soon?" answered the nearest.

"Where's your partner?" asked the other.

I didn't allow them to do any more thinking or talking. A long, looping kick landed in the pit of the first guerrilla's stomach. I used the rifle butt on the other one's chin to take him out. It might have been quieter using my stiletto. The crunch of bone against wood stock sounded like a gunshot in the still night.

Waiting to see if any in the camp a few yards away had heard, I fingered the trigger of the AK-47. When no one came to investigate, I began searching through the supplies. I didn't care what I came up with as long as it pointed directly to the Soviets. A few tins of food with Russian cyrillic lettering, an instruction manual for field sanitation and a three-week-old copy of their Army newspaper, *Red Star,* all went into my knapsack. Stooping to steal the two guards' rifles, I felt I had a complete set of evidence for a frame-up.

I jogged all the way back to where I'd left Dasai and Ananda. Along the road, I dropped the copy of *Red Star,* a page from the field manual, a few unspent AK-47 rounds along with the empty cartridges I'd already picked up in the road and finally the tins of food. I was famished but the thought of eating Russian food didn't thrill me. The unsanitary way in which it was prepared would give me the runs for a month.

"Where have you been, Nick?" Ananda questioned, sincere concern in her voice.

"Been doing a little shopping. And now it's time to do a little convincing. When was the last sentry by?"

"Less than ten minutes," Dasai responded. "Another will not be by for a half hour or more."

"Great." I unlimbered one of the heavy AK-47s, pulled the slide back and let the snick echo out into the night. It sounded as loud as any gunshot. I repeated the action several times, leaving unspent shells all around. Then I lifted the muzzle into the air and started firing short, choppy bursts.

When the gun jammed, I tossed it down, picked up the second and motioned for Ananda and Dasai to follow. I fired as I ran, hoping it appeared that dozens of snipers lurked out in the dark. Answering fire came, accurate, deadly. I kept firing into the air, into the ground, into outbuildings, until the second AK-47 came up empty. I immediately discarded it and began spraying the third rifle's slugs in a wide path through the main street of the Sikh village.

I waited long enough to see a tight knot of turbaned men rush into the open. I fired carefully, not wanting to injure any but definitely wanting them to get the idea that they might die if they didn't fight. I dropped the last of the supplies I'd stolen from the guerrillas, then began firing as accurately as I could with the bulky rifle.

When this third AK-47 also jammed, I tossed the weapon aside and motioned to Dasai and Ananda to run like the very wind. I followed, Wilhelmina in hand. I didn't want to use any of my precious 9mm slugs; it wasn't necessary. The swift ambush inside the Sikh village had taken them by surprise. The Sikhs had quickly responded to having lead tossed about their ears and figured their return fire had driven off whoever was so bold and foolish to attack.

When we found a secure spot atop a small rise about two kilometers from the town, we collapsed, gasping for air.

In a few minutes the Sikhs began a rising and falling chant that sent cold ripples down my spine. They'd found the AK-47s. They'd found the tins of food. And they were on the trail I'd left of discarded Russian artifacts, following them like Hansel and Gretel intended following their dropped bread crumbs out of the woods.

The Sikhs marched to do battle. A slow smile crossed my face. It had been a good night's work, after all.

TWELVE

The shrill whistling was all too familiar.

"Incoming mortar shell!" I cried, pulling Ananda down beside me and trying to protect her. Gupta Dasai had already gone to ground, sliding behind a large rock outcropping. The mortar round hit and exploded less than twenty yards away. Dust and bits of flying rock cascaded down; the mortar shell fragments had missed us.

I peered up over a small boulder and down into the valley where the Sikhs and the Russian guerrillas fought fiercely. My plan worked almost too well. I'd started a pitched battle that didn't appear close to being over.

The Sikhs hadn't taken kindly to having their homes riddled with bullets. Their strategic and tactical sense must have been innate for such a well-executed mission against the Russians to have been put together on such short notice. Their leader split his forces into a pincers movement, cutting off any hope of retreat for the guerrillas. Only then did the Sikhs attack.

And it was without quarter.

I watched the progress of the battle through my binoculars. In a way I felt like a small child who had found a gun with a hair trigger. I'd almost innocently touched the trigger and gotten an explosion far outweighing anything I'd expected.

The guerrillas were cornered and had nowhere to run. They fought like trapped rats. I'm sure their commanders had told them it was all right coming into the country as guerrillas, that there wouldn't be any opposition to speak of. If there was, the helicopter gunship would take care of it. With the Sikhs hot to slaughter, no amount of air support would help. Even if the Russian guerrillas called in their chopper, much of the fighting was hand to hand. They'd kill as many of their own men as they did of the enemy with an air strike.

"I do not believe it," said Ananda. "The Sikhs fight the Russians."

"All they needed was a good reason," I said. "I hadn't intended for them to be this thorough about it. They've sealed up the valley on both sides of the guerrilla camp. In fact, I think they might even have sealed it up behind us."

"They have," confirmed Dasai, after slowly scanning the dawn-lit terrain at our backs.

"We're as bottled up here as the Russians. I'd wanted to move further north, toward the Khyber Pass, and see what the situation was there."

"The Shinwari tribesmen control all trade through Afghanistan," said Ananda slowly, as if thinking out loud. "They might allow the Russians entry. If so, the Khyber Pass is no place for any of us."

"I've got to check," I said. "My boss needs all the information he can get on this place."

"You said your radio was destroyed. How will you communicate?"

I shrugged. There were all sorts of ways an inventive field agent can get word back to home base. AXE maintained one of the best communication networks of any organization in the world. Even a simple pay telephone could get me patched through to Hawk, wherever he was in the world. Unfortunately, the Khyber Pass area didn't have any. Still, there were ways. All I'd have to do was find one.

"Look, watch this!" cried Dasai.

The Russian guerrillas tried to break through and get back into friendlier territory. It didn't work. The Sikhs might not have had as modern equipment, but they had the will and temperament to fight. And fight they did.

The slaughter hardly pleased me, but the guerrillas got what they deserved. I remembered Dasai's village lain waste because it stood in the way of further conquest.

A familiar sound of that particular battle came back to me—then I realized I wasn't remembering, I was hearing. The sound of helicopter blades wracked the air.

"They come to kill the Sikhs," said Ananda. "Just as they did with us Muhmands."

"I'm afraid so," I said. There wasn't any way of warning the Sikhs. They'd have to find out the hard way what it meant for poorly armed peasants to run counter to modern weapons. In helpless rage I watched as the huge gunship came into view, then hovered as its crew studied the battle below. I figured this was the time they'd use their chemical weapons. Poison gas would sweep through the valley, killing plants and animals as well as humans. The guerrillas probably had gas masks in their equipment bags. It might take them a few minutes getting into their gear, but the mycotoxin nerve gas would eliminate the problem of Sikh and guerrilla being close by.

What happened then astounded me because it was so unexpected. From a distant hill where the Sikhs had one of their observation posts I saw a bright glint of reflected metal. Then a long cylinder of flame erupted skyward. The helicopter didn't have a chance. The heat-seeking, ground-to-air missile ran right up the gunship's exhaust. For a moment two suns blazed in the morning sky. Then one, of molten metal and fused human bodies, twisted slowly and fell to earth.

"A rocket," I said. "The Sikhs used a hand-held launcher to knock down the chopper."

"Where did they get such a weapon?" Ananda asked.

"It might be Russian. Could they have captured some Soviet equipment in a prior skirmish, or possibly have traded for it?"

"Perhaps," said Dasai. "The Sikhs are not ones to waste anything. That is why their Golden Temple in Amritsar is so magnificent."

The Sikhs would have something special to pray over during prayers. The helicopter hadn't had time to use any of its toxic gases. By knocking it down in flames, they destroyed most of its weapons, chemical and conventional.

"Let's try and get past their guards before the commotion dies down," I said. The Sikhs still worked on isolated pockets of Russian resistance. It wouldn't be twenty minutes before they finished their battle by totally eliminating the guerrillas.

We worked our way down the valley, along a ledge Dasai had found and past the guerrilla encampment far below us. I felt exposed walking along this aerial pathway. Any below us looking up would spot the three of us immediately. With the Sikhs so fired up and hot-blooded, it struck me as approaching impossible that we could escape this easily.

We topped a rise and started down a winding, rocky path when bullets ricocheted all around us. From their direction, we weren't caught in a cross-fire. If we had been, the Sikhs would have finished us off in seconds.

"Go left, Dasai, Ananda," I ordered, even as I worked my way to the right. Ananda started to argue but her brother saw my plan and pulled her with him. I didn't think we faced all that many men, possibly no more than three. The majority of the forces still fought in the valley. If our luck held—karma—there would be only a solitary rifleman.

A trail of bullets followed Dasai and Ananda. I holstered Wilhelmina in favor of a more silent kill. From the timber of the gunshots, we faced a Sikh with one of the Afridi rifles and not a Russian with an AK-47. If at all avoidable, I wanted to keep from killing. The more Sikhs left alive in the valley, the more there were to fight off future Soviet incursion. Forcing the Russians to find another path into the heart of Pakistan and India had to set their timetable back.

A delaying action was the best I hoped for.

A pale purple turban was my first sight of the sniper. He rose enough for me to see a heavy, dark beard and curly hair poking out from the back of the turban. He wore a black *sherwani*. That made up my entire impression of him before I got my feet gathered and dived onto his broad back. The force of my body hitting him carried us both forward, his rifle left behind.

With the strength and agility of a lion, he twisted in my grip and kicked out. I went flying, rolled and came to my feet facing him.

"I am Raj Singh," he said. "Know your killer, Russian cow eater."

I didn't bother correcting him about my not being a Russian. All I saw was his six-foot-five frame moving with controlled liquid grace. The strength hidden under the long coat became apparent when we again grappled. I knew there wasn't much chance of outpowering him. Skill would have to prevail if I were to walk away from this alive.

Unfortunately, his skill matched mine. Every trick I tried he easily countered. His blows slowly wore me down; in a battle depending on stamina, he had the edge. I'd been going for almost twenty-four hours without food or much sleep and the altitude sucked much-needed oxygen from my lungs. Exertion told on me more than it did the Sikh, who had been born to this height.

The irony of being killed by someone I counted on as being friendly wasn't wasted on me.

"*Aieee!*" he shrieked. His bull-like attack presented the most minute of openings for me. With speed and precision, I caught his right wrist, turned into him and sent the heavy body flying over my hip in a neatly done *seionage* shoulder throw. I hung onto his sleeve to keep him from getting away and drove my elbow straight down into his forehead. The soft purple turban cushioned the blow a bit, but enough force remained to knock him out.

"Nick?" came Ananda's anxious call. "Are you all right?"

"Fine," I said, panting. "Let's get out of here before Raj Singh wakes up."

Dasai stared at the fallen Sikh, then at me.

"He is their champion," he said. "The name Singh denotes a title of champion or lion. And Raj . . ."

"Raj," I said, piecing it slowly together, "means king. King Lion."

"Their best," said Ananda in a weak voice. Her eyes widened as she, too, realized I'd met their best in hand-to-hand combat and won.

"Let's check on the Shinwari," I said, "and ask what it costs to let through a Russian guerrilla unit."

We turned toward the distant Hindu Kush Mountains and began walking. My job had just begun.

THIRTEEN

We made good time. We had to. The thought of Raj Singh's anger when he came to wasn't too pleasant to consider. I found myself becoming more and more taken with the scenery of the country. We remained in Pakistan, taking a narrow panhandle north and west up toward the Khyber Pass. We avoided the vagrant tribesmen wandering the corridor as much out of caution as anything else. I had the uneasy suspicion many of these tribesmen aided and abetted the Russians, either knowingly or otherwise. From what Dasai had told me, the Shinwaris had to allow the guerrillas through the Khyber Pass. Maybe they were paid off, maybe there was something else happening. I'd find out.

But getting past Fort Jamrud inside the pass undetected wasn't possible—both Gupta Dasai and Ananda told me so. I'd take their word for it, for the moment.

There didn't seem any other way the helicopter gunship could have gotten onto this side of the pass undetected, either. The high mountains made it impossible to fly over. The maximum operating altitude for a heavily armed and armored helicopter is about twelve thousand feet. Stripped down and turbo-powered, sixteen thousand is the maximum, and that's pushing the equipment to the limit.

Some of the *passes* further up in the Hindu Kush from Afghanistan were over eighteen thousand feet in altitude. Unless the guerrillas brought the copter over piece by piece, only the Khyber Pass looked plausible.

The majestic mountains climbed sharp, knife-edged and breathtaking all around us, forming a stony necklace about the land. The valley tightened as we went along, leaving little more than a roadway to walk. We found it increasingly difficult avoiding others traveling the road until we were within a few miles of the Khyber Pass.

A large valley spread forth, almost like a green tablecloth dropped on the barren rock. Grass grew in profusion here and the brown ribbon of road fed into blacktopped highway leading into the Khyber Pass. I didn't have to be told this was the entrance. Through my binoculars I spotted the heavily armed bands milling around the mouth of the pass. Less than a mile through the twenty-seven mile long pass stood Fort Jamrud, that bristling fortress built by the British.

Getting past that commanding fort required the ability to turn into a ghost. No helicopter gunship sneaked past.

"Why would the Shinwari allow the Russians into this country? Don't they know what will happen?"

"The Shinwari tribe does not have the sense of honor others do. Individuals among them would deal with the Russians, even allowing through the helicopter," said Ananda. "Their family sense is weak. No single man rules an entire family. They argue often, fight much."

"The *badal* retaliation is constant among them," added Dasai. "They control all trade in the Khyber Pass. Their power is great, if you desire to leave Afghanistan or enter it."

Kabul, Afghanistan, lay a mere two hundred miles from our position—through the Khyber Pass, down the slopes of the mountain, across treacherous desert and then into the valley at the base of the Hindu Kush cupping Kabul like a gem in a bowl. But I didn't have to go to Kabul. My problems lay closer to hand.

"Money is all it takes to bribe the Shinwari?"

"Money means little in this country," said Dasai. "But food." He shrugged.

"Food, clothing, medicine, those things can buy much in the way of negligent sentry duty," said Ananda. "Do you blame them so much? You have seen life is harsh in the mountains. The capitals of Islamabad and New Delhi are distant; the rulers care little for the top of the world. We get by however we can."

I listened with half my attention. The rest focused on a small village a few miles away, well back from the mouth of the Khyber Pass. Two Russian-made jeeps were parked in front of a house. From behind the same house I saw a hood of a much larger truck. While I couldn't be sure, I thought a large antenna rose up from the roof. The truck and jeeps were large enough to crate over a helicopter. This might be the Russian guerrilla commander's base.

"Down there," I said, pointing out the vehicles and radio antenna. "Do you know whose house that is?"

Neither did.

"I'm going to do a little spying. That's too blatant an invitation to pass up. You both stay here and I'll rejoin you in a few hours. Rest up, if you can."

"I am hungry, Nick," Ananda said.

I realized I was feeling a little weak myself from lack of food; we hadn't eaten in thirty-six hours. "Go on," I told her. "Get what you can, but be careful. There's no way to tell who's our friend here and who's in the pay of the Russians." I realized how paranoid that sounded. The way she looked at me made me want to take her in my arms and kiss her, but I refrained. With her brother so close by, it didn't seem proper.

"We will eat only when you return. We are used to our stomachs grumbling."

"Eat when you can, but save me a little," I told her. "There's no telling how long this recon might take." I didn't want to add that there might be no returning if I were caught.

I set off at a brisk pace, traversing the hill and finding a dirt path curling around its base. On relatively flat ground, making my way through tended fields, I slowed down and became more cautious. If the Russians operated openly in this area, their patrols would spot me immediately if I stayed on the roads. Parking jeeps out in plain sight meant one of two things: total disregard of secrecy or total control. I had to believe the Soviet commander had the area fairly well subdued.

That explained the helicopter gunship, the guerrilla band working down the valley and everything I'd seen so far around here.

They were further along in forming their base to attack Pakistan and India than I'd dared think.

I fought off buzzing flies as I approached the house spotted earlier. A large whip radio antenna rose from the roof. In the back several native-dressed men worked on assembling a three-meter-diameter microwave dish antenna. The Soviets have several geosynchronous communications satellites in orbit high over the Indian Ocean. With the high mountains blocking radio communication, even to Kabul only two hundred miles away, this microwave ground station gave them the capacity to receive signals sent from Moscow, East Berlin or Kabul via the satellite.

Avoiding the workers wasn't too difficult a task. They were intent on their project and one of the jeeps had been parked close enough to the house to provide cover. I did a quick dash, skidded under the jeep and pressed myself against the cold stone wall of the house. Moving carefully, I snaked upward until I heard voices coming through a chink in the rock. Using Hugo, I enlarged my peephole.

A Russian colonel sat in a chair with his back to me. The sounds from inside came intermittently but gave enough detail that I knew the big Soviet push wasn't going to be long in coming.

When the colonel turned and I saw his profile, I cursed low and long. It was Arkady Suslovitch, a brilliant commander. Colonel Suslovitch's voice rose until I heard every word he said.

"Major, we went to considerable effort getting the gunship over. What do you mean we've lost contact with it?"

"Sir!" the frightened voice came. The major stayed beyond my limited vision. "There is no report from the ground force, either."

"No word at all?" Suslovitch's words were deceptively soft. From his reaction, the major felt each and every one as a whiplash across his naked back.

"No, sir!" There came a coughing, as if the major tried to regain control.

"Lieutenant Marko, please remove him. Have him listed as missing in action. No, not that. Put the major in for a medal. The Order of Lenin or something similar. He had powerful connections in the Kremlin."

"With the KGB, sir," came the lieutenant's voice. "With Comrade Andropov himself."

"Quite right. Anyone connected with the chief of the KGB does not die less than a hero's death. And please see to finding out where our gunship has gone." Under his breath he added, "I cannot stand incompetence."

"Right away, sir!"

I knew Colonel Arkady Suslovitch all too well. He left nothing to chance. His planning was meticulous, his execution painstaking. His headquarters wouldn't be left unguarded. I'd lucked out getting in so easily. The Soviet High Command had done well choosing him for their commander on this sensitive mission. If anyone in their service could pull off a supposed guerrilla uprising that eventually brought New Delhi to ruin, it was this man.

I slipped back down under the jeep when I heard rusty hinges opening. The lieutenant came out, personally dragging the major. The major was quite dead, his throat cut. Arkady Suslovitch preferred to use a knife to a pistol, I remembered. His AXE dossier hadn't been updated for almost two years. He had dropped out of sight, presumed dead.

Hawk needed to know one of the Soviet's most capable commanders headed the drive down into Pakistan, and I had no way of getting that information through to him.

FOURTEEN

Eyeing the radio antenna above the house, I thought that my problems might be nearly solved. No matter that Arkady Suslovitch was inside, and with him several dozen armed Soviet soldiers masquerading as guerrillas. The radio meant everything to me.

I remembered the exterior arrangement of the antenna and lead-in wires and decided the radio unit had to be in a room on the far side of the house. Staying outside and risking one of the technicians working on the microwave link spotting me seemed suicidal, so I forced open a low window and slithered over the sill to the floor inside.

The furniture in the adjoining room hardly made up for the lack in the one I'd entered. Peering around the corner of the door, I saw a single desk and chair where the Russian colonel had sat. One straight-backed wooden chair faced the desk. Small droplets of drying blood spotted the front of the desk, the only evidence that the major had been removed permanently from the staff. A kerosene lantern sat on the floor and that was all. I wondered where Suslovitch had gone.

My chances of being caught increased as I explored further. Voices came from the far side of the house. Moving down the hall, I stopped and listened outside the door. Static popped and hissed. A radio had been turned on.

"The destroyer in the Indian Ocean has picked up our

signal, sir," came the brisk tones of the radioman.

"Code Four."

"Code Four being used, sir."

"Mission on schedule. Six days until full strength. Send tanks immediately." Suslovitch heaved a deep sigh and said to the radioman, "The die is cast. Our tanks will arrive very soon, maybe less than a week. Then we go to Karachi."

"Yes, sir!" the radioman said appreciatively. I didn't blame him. Being in the Pakistani port, fighting or not, had to be better than garrison duty at the top of the world.

I ducked into another of the deserted rooms off the hall and let Colonel Suslovitch pass. He was close enough for me to reach out and touch the gold epaulettes on his uniform. The temptation to remove this dangerous man from the game once and for all seized me, but I had a higher duty at the moment. I had to report to Hawk. That took precedence over anything else.

The radioman worked diligently at transmitting the encoded message. I waited, hoping he'd leave the room after he'd finished informing the Kremlin of Suslovitch's readiness. I noted that Suslovitch hadn't been totally frank with his superiors. The loss of the gunship had to be a real setback, yet the colonel was brilliant enough to be able to make the incursion without it. I stood in the hallway, getting more and more nervous about being seen. The radioman finished his official message, then picked a new frequency. He began another conversation, this time a personal one.

"My darling, it's been such a long time," he said.

A female voice crackled over the rig, giggling girlishly, replying, "Oh, Dmitri, it's only been a few hours."

"They have been centuries for me."

I cursed my bad luck. The radioman had a sweetheart, also probably in the Soviet Army, with access to a radio. This might go on for hours until some official communiqué came through.

I acted.

Slipping into the room, I closed the door. The

radioman's expression was one of true lust. He was lost in a fantasy conversation with his girl friend. He never knew what hit him. I slugged him behind the right ear with the butt of my Luger.

At least one thing was to my favor. He hadn't turned off the transmitter after sending Suslovitch's message. I didn't need to warm the rig up again. I cut off the woman by spinning the frequency selector to one I was sure would get through to a comsat poised high over the Indian Ocean and often used by AXE agents in the Asiatic sector.

I fine tuned until a tiny beeping sounded. That was the okay to transmit signal. I began.

"N3, from a hostile transmission point," I explained, after giving my clearing code sequence.

"Go ahead, N3," came Hawk's voice. I guessed it was almost four A.M. Washington time, yet Hawk sounded as alert as he would at four P.M.

"Arkady Suslovitch is commanding. He's ordered tanks sent through the Khyber Pass to arrive within a week. His helicopter gunship has been destroyed." I didn't bother explaining how. It wasn't pertinent to my report. "Current guerrilla forces on the Pakistani side, number unknown. He stands a good chance of making the incursion succeed, in spite of strong local opposition. There are other corridors down into the Pakistani heartland he can use. Shinwari tribesmen controlling the Khyber Pass have been bought off, bribe used unknown."

"Very good, N3. Pictures?"

"Gear lost, sir. The village I stayed in has been destroyed."

"I see."

"Orders?" I didn't know if I wanted to hear what Hawk had to say on this or not.

"Stop them, N3. However you can."

"It's me against at least a company, perhaps a full battle group."

"I know, N3. Slow them down. We have the State Department together with the Pakistani ambassador.

He remains unconvinced of Soviet activity. Our satellites will try to pick up the tanks."

"Any chance of getting the Pakistanis to send a small company of troops up to check this out?"

"Not really." The hiss and pop of static was the only indication of the fifteen thousand miles separating us.

"I'll do what I can, sir."

"I know you will, N3. Good luck."

"Thank you. N3 out."

I shut down the transmitter, then tinkered with its innards for a while, removing the thyratron and a couple of leads to the power supply. The power tube I smashed, the rest I left. It only inconvenienced, not prevented. Right now, even a slight irritation might be good enough to slow the Russian advance.

I didn't believe that for an instant, not with Colonel Suslovitch commanding, but I needed some faint ray of hope.

The radioman stirred. I felt sorry for him, both because I'd interfered so with his love life and because Arkady Suslovitch might have him taken out and shot. I doubted the radioman had KGB connections; his family wouldn't even get a posthumous Order of Lenin. I slugged the man again to keep him from calling out.

Then I did a fade. Through the door, down the hallway, seeking out Colonel Suslovitch. Before, reporting to Hawk had taken top priority. Now that my orders were to slow the Soviet advance in whatever way I could, taking out Suslovitch seemed the likeliest course.

The colonel provided the key to success. He had just murdered his second in command for sloppiness. I doubted that Lieutenant Marko would be given command of such an important mission. Remove Suslovitch, stop the incursion until a new field grade officer could be sent.

Wilhelmina in hand, I stalked Suslovitch.

This time the Soviet officer had left and was nowhere to be seen. I hurriedly searched the rest of the large house and found nothing of interest. The few reports in the desk were trivial. Suslovitch obviously moved fast and light, not wanting to leave behind much to implicate the Russians should their ploy fail. A cautious man, Arkady Suslovitch.

I sat on the edge of the desk, thinking hard. As it stood, Suslovitch was the only one I'd seen in Soviet Army uniform. The rest dressed in gear suitable for guerrillas. The real evidence indicted the Kremlin, but the soldiers themselves looked like Peoples Revolutionary Freedom Fighters, or whatever the current popular name for Soviet aggression was. In a short while, Suslovitch would also be in mufti.

Scouting around, I looked out the windows. In the front, Suslovitch stood with his lieutenant watching the "guerrillas" drill in close order. Out back, the technicians still worked putting up the satellite dish. I considered a single long shot at Suslovitch, then discarded it. If I hit him, fine. My job was done, and it didn't matter what happened to me. On the other hand, he presented a difficult target. Fail to kill and I'd tipped my hand and my usefulness to AXE and the cause of world peace was gone.

I left the house, found a ravine and made my way back toward the spot where I'd left Gupta Dasai and his sister. All the distance I worked over possible plans, possible techniques. Even when I reached the small camp where Ananda cooked vegetables in a small pot, I hadn't come up with any good scheme.

Pakistan faced a well-equipped, superbly commanded guerrilla force. All I had were a Luger and a knife, a Hindu woman disgraced because her husband had been killed by the Russians and her brother, ex-mayor of a minuscule mountain village.

The odds against success were as high as the Hindu Kush.

FIFTEEN

"I need a rifle. Not one of the old Martini-Henry single shots, either," I said. "Something with a telescopic sight." The idea of plugging Suslovitch from a distance still seemed my best bet, but I needed an accurate rifle for such sniper work.

"There is no such thing in these mountains," said Dasai. "The tribesmen all cherish their rifles, but they are poor weapons. Many of the Afridi are excellent marksmen."

I didn't doubt that. I didn't doubt, either, that they'd be world class competitors—and assassins—with top of the line rifles.

"Why must you kill the Russian colonel?" asked Ananda.

"I don't have to kill him specifically, though I certainly want to." I didn't explain to her how deep my feelings ran against Colonel Arkady Suslovitch. I had run afoul of him before, years ago, when he'd been a captain stationed in Hungary. He'd been assigned to Warsaw Pact maneuvers planning, in Red Army Intelligence: the GRU. I'd been dropped in to retrieve some plans he worked on concerning possible avenues of tank attack through West Germany. NATO needed those plans to do some strategic work of their own. I had stolen the plans, but not before Suslovitch personally saw to it that the entire AXE apparatus in Hungary was eliminated. Along with two agents who had nothing to do with the theft of the plans, he took out a very good friend of mine.

Seymour Hengeist had been a small man, a mousy-looking fellow who jumped at his own shadow. That act kept him alive through tough times. He was a crack shot, a top judo-ka, and used piano wire garrotes like he'd invented them. We'd worked together on several projects over the years and I respected him greatly.

His greatest asset was not looking like a spy. That hadn't confused Arkady Suslovitch for an instant. Sy died to allow me the chance to escape with the documents I'd taken. I'd lost a good friend.

The reasons I had for taking out Suslovitch were as much personal as professional.

"If there is another way of stopping the Soviet guerrillas, would you take it?" asked Dasai.

"What other way?" I asked bitterly. "The Shinwari can stop them, but they've been paid off. They're even allowing tanks through the Khyber Pass."

"We have seen much of the Soviet troops below," said Dasai, tapping my battered binoculars. "The destruction of our village is only the beginning, isn't it?"

"Only the beginning," I assured him.

"We need to speak with the Old Man of the Mountains."

"You've mentioned this 'Old Man' before," I said. "In connection with the goddess Kali."

Dasai nodded solemnly, as if I'd invoked a powerful living deity. "The Old Man is Kali's right hand. He guides her worshipers. I do not believe that the Old Man of the Mountains will allow the Russians to take over Pakistan."

"What does he have to offer?" I asked. I was willing to try anything.

"His power is immense, far reaching," said Ananda. "The goddess Kali provides for her own."

Kali was another of the Hindu polytheistic manifestations. One god or goddess had as many as nine different forms. Kali was one of the aspects of Shiva the Destroyer's bride. I vaguely recalled the goddess' worshipers—

the so-called thugs—giving the British seven kinds of fit in the middle of the last century. Maybe there were a few devotees to *thuggee* still around and they were controlled by this Old Man of the Mountains both Gupta Dasai and his sister talked about in almost reverential tones.

"The Old Man is special. He heads the cult devoted to Kali. He is the ruler of the northern part of Pakistan."

"I'm sure this comes as a surprise to the government."

"Why do you not see government troops stationed here? How do you think a Hindu sect survives here?" asked Dasai. "It is no secret who rules."

"Why even allow the Russians into the country in the first place?" I countered. "We might be going from bad to worse. If the Old Man of the Mountains is permitting the Russians in, we'd be sticking our necks into a noose going to beg help."

"He knows," said Ananda. "He is unaware of the danger. He is an ascetic and sometimes out of touch with political reality."

They had almost convinced me this mythical person existed. I found myself thinking in terms of men, arms, logistics, forced marches, sweeping strategies. Then I shook out of it. There wasn't any Old Man of the Mountains. If there was, he certainly didn't have the power Dasai and Ananda attributed to him.

"Does he control the Shinwari?" I asked.

"He allows each tribe to worship in their own manner. This is the way of Hinduism. Kali is but one manifestation of the godhead. He even permits the Sikhs to remain."

I had to laugh at that. No one *permitted* the Sikhs to do anything. They were good enough fighters to do what they pleased. It still impressed me that they'd removed the guerrilla force as well as the helicopter, even if I did have to dupe them into the effort.

"Okay, you've convinced me. We go tomorrow morning to talk with the Old Man of the Mountains. Where is he?"

Gupta Dasai motioned vaguely in the direction of the Hindu Kush, to the north. I sighed. Those were tall mountains, and they covered a lot of territory. Still, the recon couldn't be wasted. I had to find other possible routes south for the guerrillas, routes able to take tanks. If I knew Suslovitch, he'd want to avoid the Sikh village altogether. Once bitten, twice shy.

The warm afternoon sun set with surprising suddenness, vanishing behind a lofty, craggy mountain. The small fire was banked behind rocks so that the Russians below couldn't see; it wouldn't matter, anyway. Hundreds of small fires winked into existence throughout the valley. We were just one more.

"Good night," I said to Ananda and her brother. They only nodded, then pulled heavy blankets around them. I had to admit their day in the valley had been more rewarding than mine, at least in terms of material goods. Ananda had found blankets and a cooking pot, while Dasai found enough food to keep us going for a little longer.

The fire died into red-glowing embers and the night chill worked its way through even the thick blanket. I dozed off, then awoke when I felt a body moving next to mine. I said nothing, opening to the cool night air until Ananda snuggled closer.

Afterwards, we drifted off to sleep, me wondering what her brother thought. Ananda's dreams weren't at all apparent to me.

Dawn came as suddenly as night had. Ananda had moved away long before, to keep the night a secret from her brother. The expression on his face let me know that nothing was a secret, at least in this regard. But Gupta Dasai said nothing. His sister had been to the West and found strange ways there; he accepted them.

We ate silently, then packed. I did a quick check of the Russian encampment and noticed nothing unusual. I wondered if Dmitri the radioman had reported the sabotage or if he'd decided to stay quiet. With Colonel Suslovitch in command, the lovestruck youngster might have been better off trying to replace the power tube and fix the damage I caused rather than reporting the incident.

"We go," said Dasai. "To the mountains."

I wanted to laugh, but by mid-afternoon I understood what he meant. I'd thought we were in the mountains. They were molehills, only tiny mounds of dirt. Once past the bowl of the green valley at the mouth of the Khyber Pass, the going became steep, rockier and exhausting.

I panted continually, gasping for air and finding none. We moved along at elevations over twelve thousand feet and still climbed. What really got to me was the Hindu Kush. It still appeared that those mountains were high, very high. But then Mt. Everest is over twenty-nine thousand feet tall—that was a good seventeen thousand feet higher than our current height.

All things considered, I decided climbing the world's highest peak wasn't what I wanted to do on my vacation. Just sloughing along and not climbing was too much like work.

"Where are the Old Man's lookouts?" I asked Dasai at the end of the rigorous day. "From the way you talked yesterday, they were all over these hills."

"They are."

"Didn't see them."

"You didn't, but they are there."

He remained aloof, as if Ananda and I were outcasts. He knew what had happened between us on the train from Lahore, or had accurately guessed. Me he discounted as a hedonistic Westerner; it was Ananda he was most angry with. She had violated cultural and probably religious morés, yet she was all the family he had left. Family ties versus moral indignation made for a fertile battleground in Gupta Dasai.

All the next day we walked. And the next. I began to worry. We went away from the Russians, away from potential attack routes. I had a good idea how Suslovitch would proceed from my first day's reconnaissance. But Dasai was intent on taking us ever higher into the mountains. I felt footweary and bone tired and ready to turn around when a stone bounced onto the path.

I twisted to look upward. A man dressed in the ornate *kurta* shirt favored by the Shinwari stood atop the huge rock, ancient rifle cradled in his arms. His mahogany face showed as much expression as the wood it resembled.

"They have found us," said Dasai.

I realized then that the pebble had been no accident. It had been a warning. Slight scraping noises on the trail behind us told of men, lots of men—and I hadn't seen a single one before they chose to reveal themselves. They blended into the hills so well that even my keenest senses hadn't detected them.

"We go to the Old Man of the Mountains," said Gupta Dasai.

It looked more as if we were being taken—as prisoners.

SIXTEEN

They followed, at least twenty armed men. As we walked, I became increasingly aware of others filtering down from the mountainside, like tiny droplets of water coalescing to form a torrential downpour. At the end of twenty minutes, I estimated a full one hundred men accompanied us. Yet, their purpose wasn't clear; no one had said a word to us.

"How many men does the Old Man of the Mountains have?" I said to Dasai, my voice barely audible above the wind howling through distant crags.

"No one knows. Many. He commands totally in this part of the world. The British often fought him—unsuccessfully. They finally came to grips with the idea that he ruled and would not disturb them in the lower portions of the country. India and Pakistan have always been ruled by many, under the guise of one."

"You talk like the current leader is the one who lived a century and a half ago." To this Dasai said nothing.

India had to be one of the most conquered nations on earth. Any would-be conqueror from Alexander the Great in the fourth century B.C. on added it to their string of conquests, something similar to a woman adding still another charm to a bracelet. Mongols and Tartars, Persians and Greeks, all had come through the Khyber Pass, down the Golden Road from Samarkand and through the Afghan Gate, to conquer. It wasn't hard to understand why anyone living in these mountains wanted to live *far* up in them. Conquest became that much more difficult.

And from the looks of our escort, conquest of this particular cult devoted to the goddess Kali might be impossible. Sure, Russia could drop an atomic bomb on the mountains, but even this didn't guarantee total control. The wind currents would blow away the fallout; the bulk of the mountains themselves would contain the blast. Only a direct hit on the Old Man of the Mountains' headquarters, wherever it was, might accomplish total subjugation.

Subjugation through genocide.

The Germans had tried it and it didn't work. I doubted if the masters of the Kremlin would go that far. Still, the lure of a warm water port might unbalance them enough to try.

I wondered what bribe the Old Man would take to oppose Arkady Suslovitch and his guerrillas.

"How much farther do we have to go?" I asked, after we'd been climbing a steep path for over an hour. No end was in sight as the stony ledge curved around a mountain.

"Who knows?" answered Ananda. "Few ever attempt to talk with the Old Man. We might be the first in a hundred years. Little information on these people gets out."

"But you said he controls most of northern Pakistan." I didn't understand what she meant.

"By fear. When your every waking moment is filled with dread and your dreams are haunted by monsters worse than reality, no one need stand over you. The Old Man of the Mountains inspires fear. His thugs control absolutely."

I got the idea. Extortion. Only a killing here and there was required to maintain order. The fear of the unknown proved more potent than the most strict police force. If the Old Man of the Mountains had to send a dozen killers a year out to enforce his dictates, it'd probably be a busy year.

"Tell me about Kali," I said to Ananda.

"The British did not approve," she started. "In 1830 they began an effort to drive out all worshipers. In ten years all they succeeded in doing was moving the worship of Kali from the lowlands into the mountains. The *thuggee* ranged far and wide, killing and maiming in the name of the many-armed Kali. They dealt in fear, lived by extortion. Their activities were echoed around the world. The goddess is a bloody-handed one, too, demanding sacrifices often."

"Great, a cult devoted to killing. And we're in their territory." I unobtrusively touched the butt of Wilhelmina. She stayed in her holster. With eight rounds, I couldn't even put a dent in the men surrounding us. More than two hundred now stalked along behind us. It was as if the rocks themselves leaked humanity. More joined us as we continued up the impossibly steep, narrow pathway.

I chanced to look over the edge. At least a mile of empty space before solid ground. A touch of vertigo hit me. I wobbled and turned in to the mountain. The solid stone reassured me. I hoped the rocky ledge we walked over stayed put. I didn't like the idea of trying to sprout wings on the way down.

"Over fifty peaks are higher than twenty-three thousand feet," Ananda went on, not noticing my momentary lapse. "Kali rules all of them, throughout the Hindu Kush. Mount Kailas, that one over there in the Himalayas, is sacred to us. It is the Mountain of Precious Snow and holds the thrones of all our gods and goddesses."

I did a quick guess as to the height of that little hill. Easily over twenty-eight thousand, it was a worthy home for even the most discerning of deities.

"Kali rules it, too?"

"No, Brahma, Shiva, others, all are there. Kali is only one aspect."

Again, the polytheism confused me. Each god had many faces, depending on the worshiper. Kali was one side of a more complex goddess. I put that aside. It didn't really matter what these people thought Kali was—what mattered were the worshipers themselves.

If the Old Man of the Mountains turned out a welcoming party this large for three tired, hungry travelers from the "lowlands," he might be able to give the Russians an even bigger surprise.

"Will we ever get to the top of this mountain?" I asked. "It goes on forever."

"We are nearing the Old Man's village," said Dasai. He pointed. I shook myself. It had to be oxygen starvation that I hadn't noticed earlier. The tricky stone path plastered to the side of the mountain had turned into a fitted block road. This kind of effort at this altitude wasn't made unless something important was nearby.

We turned around the side of the mountain a few more times, then came to a large plain. I stopped and simply stared. Immense time and wealth—and lives—had been spent leveling the plain. Even more had gone into the ten-story high carved stone pillars on either side of a five-story wooden gate. Demons and gods had been carved into the wood, giving it a surreal look. In the stone pillars supporting the tons of wooden gate were silver and gold chasings. A hard jab from behind got me moving again. People swarmed out of the hillside, like bees from a hive. By the time we reached the gates and felt suitably awed and diminished, over a thousand people milled behind us.

"I've never seen anything more beautiful," I said, studying the artwork on the gates and pillars.

Every breath I took strained me to the utmost. The altitude robbed me of all but forty percent of the air I'd expect at sea level. If I hadn't been in good shape to start with, I'd be gasping like a fish out of water. As it was, I merely panted.

"We must enter," said Dasai, fear beginning to come into his voice.

"So?"

"The inscription on the gate reads 'Praise the Goddess Kali, Worship Her With Death To Unbelievers.'"

"Strong stuff," I said, then realized that meant me. Us. I had no idea what particular sect Gupta Dasai and his sister belonged to. Hinduism was as split as the ancient Greek and Roman beliefs.

What the warning intended, I hoped, was to keep unbelievers out. The ones who weren't invited. Then I began to worry about our escort. Maybe they weren't inviting us in but rather showing us to the place of execution. We'd purposely invaded the Old Man of the Mountains' territory.

I shook off that idea. If he'd wanted us dead, there had been ample opportunity on the mountain. We'd have died and never known it. Still, from the history of Kali that Ananda had given me, the goddess was a vindictive bitch delighting in torture.

We walked through the gates. As they swung shut in a ponderous arc behind us, I felt as if I'd entered another world. Cut off, there was only one way to go—forward.

Almost a mile into the side of the mountain I had my next shock. We were on a rim overlooking the inside of the mountain. It had been hollowed out. A city bustled some thousand feet below, a complete city of at least a quarter million people. Distant torches flared and smoked, veiling the city in murk, but enough came through to impress the hell out of me. A complete civilization flourished at the top of the world, buried under an enormous mountain. I'd thought the gates and the stone pillars supporting them had been magnificent. This hollowed-out mountain and the city it contained ranked as the largest engineering project executed by man.

And it was totally unknown except to the followers of Kali living here.

"Down," came the curt command from a weathered man with bandoliers of ammunition crossing his thick chest. He carried an ancient rifle, and when I didn't move, he pointed it. The road, a superhighway in width, snaked back and forth down to the floor where the city sprawled. I began walking, Dasai and Ananda following.

I had the distinct impression this mission had gotten out of hand, that even Nick Carter, Killmaster, was in over his head.

SEVENTEEN

We walked through streets as busy as any I'd seen in Lahore or Peshawar. The people appeared no different, except that there were no Muslims here. All were Hindus, all were devotees of Kali. A full mile into the city, I turned and looked upward. The ledge on which we'd stood peering down vanished into the smoky distance. A tiny sliver of light marked the tunnel mouth leading out into the world, but that was the only indication of entrance or exit from the city.

I turned my attention to another perplexing item. Where did the light come from? Smoking torches burned along the streets, but these didn't account for the faint glow emanating from the rock itself. A cold shiver raced up and down my spine. Thoughts of natural deposits of radium so close by, the radiation zinging through my body, didn't help my peace of mind. Yet the people in the city appeared healthy enough, even if they were glum. No one smiled and the children were somber, as if they carried the weight of the world on their shoulders.

It took a paranoid religion to bury its followers under a mountain. In spite of the engineering marvels required to produce this vast city, a fanaticism beyond belief drove them. I wanted to meet with the Old Man of the Mountains, dicker for some sort of alliance between us against the Russians, then get the hell out of here.

I tried not to think of the millions of tons of rock overhead, much less the armed men on all sides.

"Here," said the talkative one. It was only the second word he'd spoken since he'd started following us on the path almost a full ten hours ago.

"Here" was a comfortable enough house, with relatively lavish furnishings and a table set with food. I almost babbled my gratitude, then held back. I nodded curtly, then motioned with my hand, as if dismissing him. This elicited the first sign of emotion I'd seen anywhere around me. He smiled, broken yellow teeth showing through his chapped, cracked lips.

Guards were posted outside the door, but it hardly mattered. Getting out of the city required an act of God—or Kali.

"Let's eat," I said. "I haven't seen a meal this enticing in weeks."

Ananda and I began eating as if this might be our last meal. Gupta Dasai sat, staring at the food as if it would bite him.

"Brother, you will need your strength. Eat," urged the woman.

Dasai had held up well under the traveling we'd done. His ribs were still tender from the shell that had grazed him, though the wound had begun to heal nicely. Most of all, he had come to grips with the reality of his situation. His psychological trauma had been worse than any physical injury. He'd lost his village, his family and friends, and had seen the beginning of the end for all of Pakistan as he knew it unless he acted to counter the Soviet takeover plans. That was heavy-duty change for a man whose only real worry before had been tending the goats.

Dasai finished and went to one of the sleeping rooms, providing hardly more than a blanket on the cold stone floor. It was obvious he left the other bedroom for Ananda and me. She eyed me significantly, but I shook my head. Gupta Dasai might not be asleep yet. Our obvious relationship had given the man enough mental pain. I didn't want to add to it without cause.

She moved closer, her thigh pressing into mine. Her

almost fragile hand rested on my arm.

"Nick, we might not have much time together."

She was right. I had no idea what the Old Man expected of us. We might be taken out and shot, or just tossed off the top of the mountain. This brief lull in the storm might give us our last opportunity to be together in a long, long time.

But duty called more strongly.

"I've got to see what's outside," I said. The look on her face was a combination of anger, fear, rejection and confusion.

"But why? We've found the Old Man of the Mountains. Isn't that enough?"

"What do you know of him?"

"He has ruled the cult of Kali for three centuries."

"Not one man. That's impossible. Is the post hereditary?"

"No, just one man, all that time. The goddess is kind to those who serve her well. She slays those who oppose her will."

I started to say something, then bit it back. Again I found the mixture of old and new in Ananda. She'd been educated in London, yet saw nothing wrong in believing that a single man might live more than three hundred years. As appealing as the thought was on a personal basis, it took on ominous meaning when the man in question headed a death cult of—how many? Half a million? There was no telling.

"I've got to find out as much as I can about him, his people, before we talk with him. There has to be a lever I can use, an argument that'll get him to cooperate."

"Kali wills all," she said. "It is karma."

"Then Kali is willing me to do a little snooping in the city. As much as I'd like to stay here with you, I've got to see what's out there." I found myself truly wanting to remain with her. There was her exotic beauty, of course, but I pushed away any thought that my feelings might run deeper than simple lust. Seeing Arkady Suslovitch had brought back painful memories of earlier times, when I'd allowed friends to enter my world. Sy Hengeist had died saving me; I still mourned for a good friend. Allowing Ananda to become more than a friend only led to further unnecessary pain on my part.

"I've got to go." I pushed her back down to the bench as she started to rise. I knew she wanted to come with me. That was out of the question.

Ananda slumped, turning back to finish her meal. With only a pang of regret, I checked the windows, the doors, the roof. There had to be a way out where the guards didn't see. A tiny opening in the roof provided my escape route. I had to suck in my gut to get through the small hole, but I made it.

On the roof, I stayed flat. I had to remember this town was similar to ones like New York City. Instead of someone higher in a skyscraper, guards might be posted along the winding road leading to the tunnel exiting the city. A full hundred stories of rocky ledge provided a lot of sentry points to observe the city.

Peering over the edge of the roof, I saw five guards lounging below. The pungent odor of marijuana floated up to me. The guards indulged in some of the usual peace-time garrison activity to pass the time. I figured they'd be stoned out of their heads for quite a while. The elevation robbed them of the oxygen needed to recover swiftly.

That same altitude kept me from performing at full capacity. As I made my way across the roofs, I had to stop frequently to allow the giddiness to pass. Forcing deeper breaths into my lungs helped a little, but if I had to go into action, my personal energy reserves were mighty slim.

As I traveled my aerial walkway I noticed a large temple in the center of town; it had to be Kali's shrine. A steady flow of people in and out proved I was right. Worshipers. They took in offerings, came out blessed.

I kept looking for some clue to guide me in my negotiations with the Old Man of the Mountains. There had to be something they needed in the city, some item of aid that the U.S. might supply. What it could be eluded me since they seemed well enough fed and clothed. Every man I saw carried at least a knife and rifle, and some even had sidearms. I decided that my best bet was to appeal to their self-interest. There had to be a reason this cult buried itself in the earth. The British attempts at eradicating the thugs of the nineteenth century only partially explained it. This was a power base for reasons other than security.

Still, I had to admire just how impregnable this fortress was. No attacking army could make it up the outside of the mountain in force. Even if the Russians dropped an atomic bomb directly on top of the mountain, I wasn't sure it had enough force to crack through the tons of rock forming the vaulted ceiling. There had been talk of the Russians developing a rock-buster bomb to destroy the NORAD Headquarters under Cheyenne Mountain in Colorado, but those rumors had never been confirmed. The technology required to build a titanium-sheathed, rocket-driven dagger carrying a nuclear device was immense. While the idea of the bomb was simple enough—at Mach 3 the titanium-nosed bomb could plow through rock with little more resistance through water—building it and delivering it were much more difficult.

So, Kali's worshipers were safe inside their stone fortress. Even cutting off the entry tunnel might not be too much of a hindrance. I suspected dozens of other entry points, all smaller, existed throughout the maze of caverns. Ventilation had to be supplied from other entrances, too, since the wind in my face entering the tunnel had been strong and steady.

I sat and watched the progress of the city until deciding that there wasn't any more information to be gained. Making my way back over the same roofs I'd used earlier, my sixth sense began to twitch and tingle. I began zigzagging, turning back on the path, using all the types of tracking lore that had worked so well for me over the years. Only once did I catch sight of a man I thought might be following me.

I sat and thought again. They'd let me out. They had followed me and knew my every movement. The Old

Man of the Mountains had let me see whatever I'd wanted—or had I seen only what *he* wanted me to see? Would the guards have recaptured me if I'd strayed into forbidden territory? There wasn't any way of knowing, or even finding out.

Disheartened, I went back to rejoin Ananda and Dasai.

EIGHTEEN

"Come," said one of the guards.

I roused myself from a troubled, guilt-wracked sleep. Ananda had wanted to do more than sleep, and I had rejected her overtures. We all needed what strength we could muster. In a way, though, I felt both guilty and sorry I'd refused her. My sleep hadn't been that good, laden with nightmares of falling rock crushing me and a multiple-armed woman coming at me, daggers in every hand. I might as well have stayed awake for more amorous and enjoyable pursuits with Ananda.

"All of us?" I asked.

"All," he said.

Ananda and Dasai solemnly fell into a single-file line behind the man. A full hundred guards surrounded us like a miniature mob. I wondered if they thought we were this dangerous or if the protection was necessary to keep the townspeople from ripping us apart. Neither answer proved satisfactory.

They had easily and unobtrusively watched me as I went on my recon expedition through the city. That proved how vulnerable we three actually were. This was their turf and they knew it intimately. Escape could only be through the tunnel, unless we accidentally discovered some other exit. So, we hardly needed a guard of one hundred armed and scowling men to keep us out of trouble.

Likewise, the populace didn't appear at all upset over

our presence. Mild curiosity was the most passionate emotion I noticed. I somehow had the feeling that any mass rally in this city had to be sanctioned by the Old Man of the Mountains himself. Anything less than complete approval spelled death, immediate and nasty.

I had trouble viewing the guards as an honor guard, too. I finally shrugged it off. Maybe this was the way it was done. Strict religions tend to do things by rote after a century or two, no matter what logic dictates.

"Where are we going?" I asked the guard.

"You know," was all the reply I got.

That had to mean we went to the shrine in the center of town. That magnificent edifice rose almost five stories and dominated the middle of the city. Huge columns hewn out of living rock supported the high roof. Creatures both mythical and real danced around those immense pillars in bas relief. In the area—almost a plain—stretching out in front of the main entrance, milled a few hundred people.

I tried to assess their mood. It was neither expectant nor angry. Everything, including emotion, was controlled in this city of Kali. The Old Man's hand was felt everywhere.

Hope began to rise for successfully arguing my case for intervention against the Russians. He had to see what menace they presented. Their atheistic views would not permit a powerful religious leader to continue, unless that leader kowtowed to them.

We made our way across the paved plain and started up the broad steps leading into the temple. At the top of the stairs, but before we actually entered, a robed man stepped out of shadow. Like mist in the morning sun, all one hundred of our guards evaporated. Watching them leave gave me an indication of how deadly a fighting force they could be unleashed against the Soviets. The Russians thought they had trained guerrillas. Kali's thugs could teach them a thing or two.

"You are Carter," said the robed man. "Ananda. Gupta. You two are favored children of the goddess Kali."

Both Ananda and Dasai reverentially bowed their heads.

"You know us," I said. "How?"

"I serve Kali. Kali knows all that happens in her mountains. When she descends from her throne on the Mountain of Precious Snow and walks the land, she notes all that occurs among her people."

"How do you know my name?" I started to add that I wasn't one of Kali's chosen, then hesitated. To point this out might spell certain death. They took their belief seriously.

"It is given us, from many sources. Your way into the mountains did not go unobserved."

"Your scouts are excellent," I said. "They can be a mighty fighting force."

"For Kali, they are invincible."

I started to ask if he was the Old Man of the Mountains, but Ananda cut me off.

"Master," she said, "we wish an audience with the Old Man. The matter is of vital importance to all who follow Kali."

"The Old Man of the Mountains is aware. He is at his daily meditation, but this will soon end and he will have received word from Kali herself."

"You know about the Russians?"

"There is little Kali does not allow us to learn. We have followed the Russian Colonel Suslovitch across the Khyber Pass. We noted with concern the flying ship pieced together with Shinwari aid. The advance of their metallic mobile forts through the pass is not unknown to us, also. Even word of the unbeliever Muslim Mujeheddin's activity inside Afghanistan reached us quickly. The death of the Russian lieutenant general has been studied."

"What? What general?" I asked. This was something that hadn't reached Western ears yet.

"General Piotr Shkidschenko was shot down in one of the flying machines. The Mujeheddin used captured Soviet rockets."

This was a major bit of information. Shkidschenko

had been commander of the Soviet forces in East Germany. Like Suslovitch, he'd dropped out of sight recently. The Russians must have moved him into Afghanistan for the purpose of taking over command of all one hundred thousand plus troops, but the Mujeheddin had shot him down before the transfer of power had occurred. This made taking out Arkady Suslovitch all the more important. If the Russians lost enough of their top-ranking personnel, they might even decide Afghanistan was growing too costly and pull out.

It wasn't much of a hope, but it was something to try for.

"Your intelligence network is superb," I complimented. "There is much we can do together."

"There is nothing we can do together," snapped the robed man. "Kali provides for all. We serve the goddess. We do as she dictates.

"But the Old Man . . ."

"He is Kali's servant, also. He is her voice on earth. We listen and follow him because he tells us what Kali wills." He turned and stalked off for the interior of the temple. Over his shoulder he tossed the curt command, "Come."

I heaved a sigh. I'd committed a major tactical blunder and insulted the man. His position seemed to be major domo, or perhaps something more like high priest, with the Old Man at the top. Whatever he was called, he obviously pulled a large number of strings and had a lot of information the West could use.

"If I've offended you, please accept my apologies."

"I cannot be offended. Only Kali is offended."

"My sincerest apologies to Kali, then."

He stopped abruptly and stared at me. It didn't take a genius to read his expression. He thought I was a complete fool. Keeping my mouth shut seemed more profitable than sticking my other foot in right now. I bowed, averting my eyes. When I looked up, the priest had continued his way into the labyrinth of Kali's temple. Ananda, Dasai and I followed, almost at a run to keep up.

We entered the main room of the temple. The marble ceiling forty feet above our heads arched with intricate paintings on it depicting the marriage of Kali and Shiva. But the ceiling was the least of the gigantic room. Fully a thousand men gathered, and the room still seemed more empty than a football stadium an hour after the game. Vast columns, so huge five men with locked arms couldn't circle, supported the ceiling. Between the dozens of columns were lined the faithful of Kali.

In the center of the room rose an altar carved from living rock. To one side was a vast pit, flames leaping and dancing in it. The amount of oil required to keep such a blaze going might have fueled half the cars in Los Angeles. To the other side was a pit, minus the fire. I didn't have to cross the forty yards and peer over the edge to know it dropped into the very center of the earth.

Dominating the room, in spite of its size and majesty, was the man in front of the altar. His presence convinced me he was the Old Man of the Mountains.

He stood with arms crossed as a small knot of ten worshipers came forth from the shadows in the far right of the temple. The man in the lead stopped, stripped off his shirt, stepped out of his pants and lifted arms upward, clad only in a short loincloth.

"Kali!" went up the deafening roar. The marble room caught the sound, created echoes, magnified it until millions of ghost voices seemed to rise.

I gasped when I saw the drama being enacted. Those accompanying the nearly naked man lifted him up and carried him forward to the pit where flames leaped a full twenty feet toward the ceiling. A complicated tripod was wheeled forth, chains and hooks dangling from the apex. The man made no sign that pain invaded his body as the cruelly barbed hooks were run into the skin on his shoulders.

The Old Man watched impassively as others began using a windlass to crank the victim up and off his feet. He hung suspended by the hooks through his shoulders. As if this weren't enough, the tripod slowly moved out to the edge of the flaming pit. The man hung from the chains as if performing a swan dive off the Acapulco cliffs. He spun slowly so that I got a good look at his face.

Ecstasy. Religious rapture totally possessed the man.

"Kali!" roared the crowd again.

The man swung out over the pit, the flames licking hungrily at his feet, his legs, his waist. The loincloth caught fire, first smoldering, then blazing into life. Those tiny flames were soon hidden by their bigger brothers coming from the bowels of the planet.

All the while he swung on the hooks, not so slowly roasting to death, he maintained the swan dive position. I watched his mahogany skin char and turn black. Blisters swelled and popped before the skin sloughed away. When the flesh of his back finally lost elasticity and no longer held him, the man fell into the pit.

He held the swan dive position the entire way.

"Kali!" shrieked the thousand men gathered.

"Kali is not a gentle goddess," said Ananda under her breath. "That man just erased much of his karma. His reincarnation will be in a much better state."

"He did that so he'd come back as a better person?" I asked, aghast at the idea of ritual, exhibitionist suicide.

"Why else? Kali favored him. Not once did he cry out. He proved his unending faith by dying."

I swallowed hard. The very qualities that made the cult members so perfect for opposing the Russians also made them perfect for insane acts such as the one I'd witnessed. Fanaticism, for whatever reason, has always remained a mystery to me. Patriotism I understand. I'm willing to sacrifice myself for my country, but I need to know that my death will serve a useful purpose. Dying to stop the Russian incursion made sense to me; if the Kremlin succeeded in their invasions of Pakistan and India, it would strain world peace to the breaking point. Western nations could no longer sit on their thumbs. They'd have to act. Red China would see the move as a pincer action and a precursor to more Russian land grabs in Asia. The obsession of Russian leaders for a warm water port had to be stopped or it would trigger a nuclear war.

That was worth dying for, if I could prevent it. If I could stop the Soviets without dying, so much the better.

But to die with barbed hooks through the shoulders while being roasted alive over an open pit, no way. That had been a senseless death, one with no purpose.

"The Old Man notices us now," said Dasai, his voice shaking with emotion.

I didn't know if I wanted to be noticed anymore.

"*Kali!*" went up the cry again.

The Old Man of the Mountains motioned us forward. A cold lump formed in the pit of my stomach. Did he demand a show of faith similar to the one we'd just witnessed before giving his considerable aid?

NINETEEN

Every step felt as if it might be my last. The gathered worshipers all fingered their rifles and knives. I had the feeling that the slightest hint of disapproval on the part of the Old Man and they'd scream and tear us apart.

They stayed back while we advanced. The quiet that had fallen was so intense, all I heard was the crackling of flames in the pit to the right and my boots clicking on the marble floor.

We stopped in front of the Old Man of the Mountains.

From a distance, he had appeared old. His white hair rippled in a breeze from some unknown duct and lines creased his face, but up close I decided he was a much younger man, no more than forty. The tough, leathery skin came from the harsh mountain weather. The white hair might have been hereditary or it might have been dyed to enhance the myth that only one Old Man of the Mountains had existed for three centuries. It didn't matter whether he had been born when the Mongols still ruled India or after World War II. He controlled these fanatics with an iron fist. Power was his.

"Carter," he said without preamble. "You come to enlist the aid of the goddess Kali against the Russian invaders."

"I do." I didn't trust myself to say more. I had no idea what the proper form of honorable address was.

"Why should the goddess Kali send her faithful to die

in such a *badal* against the *mlechchas*?"

"Barbarians," supplied Ananda in a low voice. "He wants to know why a blood feud should be declared against the Russian barbarians."

"You are able to remember the British," I said, playing on his myth of being three hundred years old. "They tried to prevent your worshipping the goddess." I pointed to a grotesque statue of Kali in the far rear of the temple. Six arms curled out from the seated figure. My mouth turned dry when I noticed that the arms all moved, slowly, sinuously. Each hand held a brilliantly polished sword or dagger. The gradual movement of the blades caught the flames from the pit and reflected back a rainbow promising not hope but death.

"I remember, as if it were only yesterday." The calm way he said that made me doubt for an instant if he didn't actually remember. Then I pushed such nonsense from my mind. This man was a consummate actor. He controlled through superstition and fear, but that didn't make him any less brilliant.

"The Russians are worse than the British. They deny all gods and goddesses."

"I am aware."

"You also know that they have weapons capable of destroying even this fabulous city of yours." I made a theatrical gesture and swept out my arms to encompass the temple, the statue of Kali, all the city.

"The goddess Kali assures us we are invincible—in her name."

"The gods war constantly," I said, sweat popping out on my forehead. "Shiva is the Destroyer. The Russians might destroy with his aid."

"If they do, then karma is served."

I hit that blank wall again. No matter what happened, it was karma. There was no changing the future, no way to alter events.

"We mean only to warn and to aid," I said, trying to change the subject. "We have seen the Russians destroyed. It is possible. You can again exist in peace."

"We live in peace now."

"It won't last!" I shouted. Calming myself, I continued at a lower level. "The Russians work to subdue Afghanistan. The Mujeheddin don't have your fighting ability. Soon they will relent and the Soviets will control the country to the north."

"The Himalayas and the Hindu Kush are Kali's. She rules, no matter what mortal nation claims the land."

Dealing with the Old Man proved more difficult than I thought. The city wanted for nothing, at least nothing the United States might furnish. Somehow, instant cameras, video games and potato chips didn't seem like much in the way of trade. Force was out of the question; I had no lever. And fear didn't work, either. These people had been sequestered so long in the mountains that they feared no enemy. The Old Man of the Mountains didn't realize the rules of the game had changed, that nations now rattled nuclear sabers, chemical weapons capable of burrowing into the tiniest of crannies, deadly biological bombs able to spread anthrax over thousands of square miles.

I felt as if I tried to explain red to a blind man.

"Do you see the menace?" I asked, trying still another tact.

"Yes."

That surprised me.

"Then act! The Russians aren't supermen. They can be defeated. One of your priests tells me of one of their leaders being killed. More can follow. Without their leaders, they will retreat." That much was true. The average Russian foot soldier came from one of the Asiatic provinces, didn't speak Russian too well and never took the initiative. Without field officers, their companies fell apart. The non-coms, for the most part, refused to accept responsibility and too many of the officers were KGB or paper shufflers—or both.

"Your plea has been heard by the goddess Kali."

I looked at him, wondering what thoughts ran through his mind. I didn't have the foggiest idea what made the Old Man tick.

"And?"

"Kali demands the dual test, one for each side of her nature."

"*Kali!*" screamed the crowd. "The test! Put them to the test!"

"What test?" I asked suspiciously, but already the surrounding warriors moved. Strong hands grabbed me. Gupta Dasai appeared at my side. And Ananda was being borne aloft on the combined efforts of twenty or more men.

They took her toward the pit on the left side of the altar, the bottomless pit.

"No!" I cried. "You can't toss her into the pit!"

"Silence." The Old Man's word came softly, yet it stung like he'd used a whip.

I watched helplessly as the same tripod that had held the barbs for the other hapless fool was brought around the altar. One small consolation: they didn't use the barbed hooks on Ananda's flesh. Instead, they were content to throw a hemp rope over the top of the tripod, then tie the end around her waist. When they finished knotting the rope, she swung out over the black pit.

The men holding me forced both Dasai and me forward. With toes on the edge of the pit, I looked down. Vertigo made me queasy. My head spun. A man beside me tossed a smoky torch into the pit. I watched as it tumbled over and over, going down and down and down. The light became a spot, a dot, a pinpoint. And still it fell. This might have been a hole to the center of the world.

Ananda dangled over the middle of the pit, held only by a thick hemp rope.

"What are you doing?" I demanded. One of the men shinnied up a tripod leg and moved to the rope, smearing something gooey onto it just out of Ananda's reach.

"You two will fight," said the Old Man, "a dozen of Kali's finest." The thugs appearing in front of the Old Man hardly looked like the best of anything, but any one of them could give me a run for the money. They were all big, strong, ugly.

"There's more," I said, beginning to understand a little about the way this devious man's mind worked.

"In this jar are hungry insects; they love the honey smeared on the rope."

It all came to me in a flash. Gupta Dasai and I had to fight our way through a dozen thugs and reach Ananda before the insects gnawed through the rope holding her. If we were killed, or were too slow, she plunged to her death in the miles deep black pit.

"What rules?" I asked.

"In a trial by will of Kali, there are no rules." The Old Man twisted the top off the jug he held. A black flight of bugs took wing, hummed around and then made an arrow-straight line for the rope. The honey proved a powerful goad for them. The rope turned black with their fighting, crawling, gnawing bodies. I fancied I saw the strands begin to part immediately on Ananda's rope.

"Fight, Dasai!" I called.

We had twelve thugs to get through, but the Old Man of the Mountains had said there weren't any rules. I still had my trusty Luger and stiletto. Wilhelmina flashed out and I fired rapidly three times, three of the thugs dying without making a sound. That no doubt increased their worthiness in Kali's eyes, but in mine dead was dead. There were three less to stand between me and Ananda. I heard a whistling sound, then felt intense pain in my wrist. The Luger fell from numbed fingers as the chain wrapped around my wrist tightened.

I spun and faced the man swinging the twenty-inch long chain. Flatfooted, I delivered a kick directly to the groin. His face blanched as he doubled up. I didn't have to worry about him anymore.

What I did worry about was getting Hugo out and into action. The spring-loaded sheath was on my right forearm. My fingers still tingled, blood refusing to flow in them again. If I tensed the muscles to send the blade rocketing downward, I'd drop it.

"Dasai, dodge, get to Ananda. I'll try to hold them off." It was bravado and nothing more on my part.

Dasai still operated at less than peak efficiency due to the injury to his ribs. I did little better. Already I wheezed and panted, trying to get enough oxygen into my starved lungs. Using my feet, kicking and moving, I rubbed my right wrist to get feeling back.

The only thing that went right for me was that none of the thugs had a pistol or rifle. All depended on nasty looking knives—and a traditional weapon which looked deceptively innocent.

I faced a man swinging a silk scarf with a large coin knotted in the center. He advanced, his movements smooth, graceful, almost as elegant as a ballet dancer. The scarf swung out, smashed into my elbow and sent a lance of pain all the way to my shoulder. That single coin was hard. But the attack didn't stop there; he moved like a tiger, getting behind me. The knotted scarf dropped, assassin-style around my throat, the coin pressing into my Adam's apple.

Less than seconds remained before I passed out.

I had to chance using Hugo. The knife shot down into my hand. My fingers trembled but held on to the cool, solid hilt. A quick upward jerk with the blade slashed through the silk scarf. A second thrust went into the thug's right eye.

The remaining men gave me no time to catch my breath.

Knives flashed, cutting fiery paths along my ribs, my shoulders and back. One long thrust opened a cut on my chin; another few millimeters lower and he'd have slit my throat.

"Dasai!" I called out. The man fought valiantly, holding off three of the remaining seven. I had to draw those men away from him; wounded as I was, I remained in better condition. A quick glance toward Ananda made my stomach knot in horror. The insects had chewed away most of the rope. She dangled by only a few fibers now.

It was a long way down into that pit.

Dropping, I kicked out letting my legs scissor shut. That toppled one man into another. The other two were on me in a flash. I felt a searing pain as one's knife cut past my ribs, then broke on the hard stone floor. He died with Hugo's point in his throat. The other hesitated. That was his downfall. My left hand picked up a fallen knife. I used it ambidextrously. Its tip hit a rib, then deflected up into his chest. My left hand became covered with his blood as I punctured his heart.

The two emerging from the heap ended up in another pile as I kicked the legs out from under one just regaining his balance. I chanced a quick knife toss; one of the men grappling with Dasai sprouted the blade in the middle of his back.

"Get to Ananda," I screamed. "The rope's almost gone."

The woman's eyes were as large as saucers as she stared up at the insects swarming over the rope. She knew better than to struggle. That put too much strain on an already weak rope. Ananda looked down into that bottomless pit, then back at the bugs. She shuddered so hard I thought that might shake off the insects.

If anything, they ate faster.

That sight drove me forward. I slashed at the pair struggling on the floor, not even caring if I severely injured them or not. I had to reach Ananda.

One of the two men left fighting Dasai abandoned his partner in an attempt to stop me. I hit him low and bowled him over. He slipped, skidded on the stone, then teetered on the brink of the pit. I kicked him in the head. He tumbled backward, his screams echoing for a long time.

I jumped onto the tripod and began climbing up one leg. I felt powerful hands pulling me back. Turning halfway, I managed to kick out and send the man reeling. Dasai, bleeding from a dozen cuts, his left arm hanging limp at his side, held off the three remaining men while I worked to save Ananda.

At the top of the treacherously tilting tripod, I reached down the rope and brushed off the bugs. Just as I touched them, I felt the strands of hemp popping faster and faster. Lunging, I grabbed the rope under the gnawed portion.

I screamed in agony as Ananda's full weight yanked down on my right shoulder. My right hand still hadn't recovered full strength, but I had to hang on no matter what. An instant's weakness on my part would send the woman plunging to her death.

"Nick, let me go. Save yourself," she said.

The blood roared in my ears. I hung on. Nothing existed in the world for me now but the pressure on my shoulder, my arm, the pain of the rope slowly slipping through my hand.

"Nick!"

I began swinging. The pain mounted, but it was the only way she'd ever be safe. The arc grew longer and longer. Finally, when I couldn't hang on another second, I let go. The agony of that release kept me from opening my eyes for several minutes.

When I finally looked, Ananda huddled on the lip of the abyss, her brother beside her. The three surviving thugs stood quietly, bleeding, probably hurting but not showing it.

I worked my way down the leg of the tripod. My feet touched solid stone. No longer was the world's mouth open under me, waiting to swallow me whole.

Weakness billowed inside. I fought back the black curtain and stood to face the Old Man of the Mountains.

He seemed neither surprised nor shocked that we had accepted this battle and won.

His next words chilled me to the bone.

"The first of Kali's challenges has been met. Prepare for the second. Immediately!"

TWENTY

My blood dripped onto the floor. I felt giddy, weak. Hugo clamped firmly in my right hand again, muscle spasms threatening to cause me to lose that precious blade. I eyed Wilhelmina lying on the stone floor some distance away. Without those first quick shots taking out three men, I might be dead—and so might Ananda and her brother. The Old Man of the Mountains had said no rules.

But the element of surprise had gone now. I didn't think I had enough strength left in me to fight a sick kitten, much less one of these leathery, tough thugs.

"The violent aspect of Kali's nature has been assuaged," he said loudly. "Prepare the arena for a softer challenge."

I didn't give a damn what he did at the moment. Let them prepare all they wanted. It gave me a chance to recoup my strength. What startled me was a woman dressed in the usual *shalwar* and *qamiz* bringing me some wine to drink. As I rolled the mountain vintage around in my mouth, she tended my wounds. Whatever this next challenge was, they didn't intend to let me bleed to death before it started.

The woman applied an astringent to the deeper cuts. The burning pain faded and a coolness replaced it. Whatever she used anesthetized and robbed the wounds of their vicious sting. I noticed that other women tended Ananda, but not Dasai. He sat to one side, trying to tend his own wounds. It was as if he had ceased to exist.

"The couch!" called the Old Man.

A half dozen men entered from the right of the temple, carrying a large round bed covered in soft furs. They placed it in the center of the temple, directly in front of the altar. I wondered about that but said nothing. My body felt halfway normal again. The young woman tending me continued to massage tensed muscles, rubbing scented oils into my skin. She also began pulling off my shirt.

That proved more of a problem than it should have. Caked blood held the fabric to my body. She didn't hurry, but soon enough the last of the blood and shirt had been scrapped off.

"Now wait a minute. That's okay," I said, when she began unfastening my pants. I looked up. A dozen men, arms crossed on massive chests, moved up and stood silently just beyond her. I got the message.

She got my pants off. Then off came my underwear. I stood buck naked in the middle of a thousand warriors.

The woman looked up at me, eyes wide and bright. Gently, she pried Hugo loose from my fingers, then massaged my wrist until all tenseness had gone. I had no idea what to expect. I began to get a hint when I saw that the woman tending Ananda had stripped her naked, too.

The Old Man stood, arms crossed on his chest, waiting. All around, people quietly went about their duties. The large bed was fluffed up. The furs on it looked like they might have been Russian sable. Ananda and I were led to stand before the Old Man of the Mountains.

"Kali is a bloodthirsty goddess; she is also a gentle goddess. You have proven yourself in combat. Now prove yourself in love!"

This was the country responsible for the *Kama Sutra*. I had never thought of that book as being the guideline for obtaining aid against the Russians, however.

"What are we supposed to do?" I glanced at Ananda, whose eyes were downcast. Gooseflesh from the cold rippled across her body. I was in scarcely better condition after my fight.

"Please Kali."

"Kali!" chanted the crowd. Over and over they chanted their goddess' name until I wanted to scream for silence.

"Nick, it's all right. This isn't the way it's supposed to be. I know. I'll be fine."

"They want us to make love? In front of all them?" I glanced back at the thousand men crowded around the perimeter of the temple. If anything, there seemed twice as many as before.

"Yes."

Tired in body and spirit, I doubted if I could fall asleep without help. To make love, and to be graded in some unknown fashion by the Old Man of the Mountains while thousands watched, didn't seem to be in the cards for me.

"I don't think I can."

"I understand, Nick." And she did. She also understood how important it was for all of us that we actually succeed. Not only wouldn't we get the legions of Kali's believers to aid us against the Russians, they would put us to death for having failed the second portion of the test. Her hand drifted down, lightly brushed my thigh, moved inward. I moaned softly as her fingers worked on me, teasing, tormenting, lightly flicking in ways designed to produce results.

Nothing. I couldn't get the thought of all those people watching out of my head.

"Concentrate, Nick, think only of me," whispered Ananda. Her hot lips moved to my ear. Her tongue flicked out and lightly traced around it. I felt her breath gusting, sensitizing, even as her fingers stroked and worked on me.

We went to the bed and lay down on it. A pneumatic wheezing told me this was a special bed. I felt as if we floated in midair, cut off from the bounds of gravity. It might be difficult for me to perform, but the test wasn't rigged. The Old Man gave every chance for success.

I tried to pull my thoughts away from those watching, from Ananda's brother sitting beside the altar, from the hideous statue of Kali, from the Old Man of the Mountains, from everything. I lost myself in Ananda's beauty. I let her kiss me all over while I wiggled in the softness of the furs.

My scarred and battered body wanted nothing more than rest. Ananda stroked and kissed until I began to respond. The silence in the temple hammered in on me. We might have been alone. I thought only of her, of pleasing her, of pleasing myself.

"Yes, Nick," she said softly. "I feel it. This is the way. Yes, oh, yes!"

I hardened until I wanted to cry. My body protested, but Ananda knew the penalty for failure. We'd both be killed, without mercy, without a second thought. My mind cast back to the time on the train, the rocking motion, the perfect, rhythmic rocking.

Her slender legs opened to me. I moved inward, sinking down into the dampness of her center. Her fingers stroked, coaxed, urged me on. Under my hands flowed soft fur, silken skin. I looked down into her dark eyes and knew that we were in the middle of the universe. Slow movements quickened. She no longer had to feign excitement to lure me on. Ananda responded; I felt her all around me.

Her fingernails cut into my back, adding new bloody tracks. Her legs gripped my waist, pulling me in. I felt her breasts, nipples firm, against my chest.

We moved together, slowly at first, then faster and faster until we merged into one being and exploded simultaneously.

"Oh, Nick," she sighed.

I blinked, sweat in my eyes. When my vision cleared, I saw a score of men standing around the circular bed. That brought me back down to the present. I extricated myself from her arms and legs and turned over, sitting up.

The Old Man stood at the altar. His expression hadn't changed. I had no idea whether our performance had been satisfactory to him or not. Beside him, leaning heavily against the altar, was Gupta Dasai. The unshed tears made his eyes seem larger than normal, like a lemur's. His world had been wracked and twisted all out of shape. He was responsible for his sister; she was all the family he had. This amounted to public humiliation for him, yet it was decreed by Kali.

Of all the people, I felt most sorry for Dasai.

The Old Man of the Mountains clapped his hands together, then finally spoke.

"The goddess Kali finds that their cause is just, that their cause is her cause. Death to the *mlechcas*. Death to the Russians!"

"*Kali!*" the cry went up, deafening me. "Kali! Kali Kali!"

War had been declared.

TWENTY-ONE

I hadn't believed it possible to mobilize the entire city so quickly for battle. Yet that's exactly what happened. Even before Ananda, Dasai and I returned to our house, the city of Kali bustled and hummed with preparation for total and complete war.

This wasn't simply war, as Westerners understand it. It was holy war. The thugs would fight to the last man. Individual glory meant nothing. Only the exaltation of Kali mattered. I saw them honing razor-sharp knives, cleaning the ancient rifles, many of which must have been made by the pervasive Afridi gunsmiths, working to gather food enough to last for weeks in the field.

In the house I sat with Ananda, my arm supporting her. The last test had taken more courage than I'd thought she possessed. If anything, she'd shown more guts than I had. When I'd wanted to quit, to give up, she had persisted. She, as much as anything else, was responsible for the success of my mission.

"How do you know they'll do as you see fit, Carter?" asked Dasai. He sat hunched in the corner, a bowl of soup in his hands. He didn't touch the food.

"I don't, but it hardly matters. They don't have to completely stop the Russian attack. All I'm hoping for is that they can slow it down so that the diplomats can argue it out. Islamabad should be responsible for sending troops to turn the Soviets back."

"You've started a holy war. The cultists won't stop

until either every single one of them is dead or the Russians retreat. From all we've heard about Afghanistan, the Russians don't quit."

"Then it's to the death on both sides," I said.

"Men armed with knives against tanks. Some battle." Dasai huddled into himself even more.

I knew why he raged so against the end result of the dual challenge the Old Man had flung at us. Fighting, Dasai understood and accepted. The more erotic challenge, with his sister and me as the main participants, bothered him greatly. He took his position as *malik,* the head of the Dasai lineage, seriously. It had required taboo breaking on his part to accept his sister back into his household when she returned a widow. To be forced to watch as a Western non-believer made love to her in front of thousands of men turned the knife already thrust into his soul.

"I know how the Russians fight, how Arkady Suslovitch is likely to form up his unit. They are under a handicap," I told the man. "The Soviets have to fight as if they were a guerrilla band, not as regular army units trained in the U.S.S.R."

"It is still knives against tanks."

"The Hungarians did very well against Soviet tanks. In these mountains, the Russians have a real disadvantage. Their diesel engines don't run as well. The fuel-oxygen mix is too heavy on the side of the fuel. This robs the tanks of power needed to get up hills."

"So we should take the high ground and wait," Dasai said bitterly.

"Yes. But there are other ways of stopping the tanks. Rocks. Explosives in cliffs above the tanks will bring down tons of rock and bury them completely. When Suslovitch sees how futile it is against a real guerrilla band—just as the Russians are finding out about the Mujeheddin in Afghanistan—they'll pull back."

"Is time all you play for, Nick?" Ananda asked.

"I play for peace. Stopping the Russians now gives a better chance at that."

"It will not be easy," Ananda said.

"This entire mess wouldn't have occurred if the Pakistanis had policed their own border. I don't understand why Islamabad doesn't have troops, lots of them, up here guarding the Khyber Pass."

"That," said a deep, sonorous voice I'd come to know and dislike, "is because Kali protects these mountains. The goddess needs no troops, other than the faithful in this city."

"The thugs?" I said, immediately hating myself for it. The Old Man of the Mountains had power in this part of the world. It didn't pay to antagonize him. But he didn't seem the least bit upset. Karma.

"Kali's followers," he corrected. "Come. We are ready to meet with the Soviet force."

"What? Already?"

"The first wave of their guerrillas begins south."

The Old Man of the Mountains turned and left, robes swirling around his ankles. I followed, dreading this. He hadn't asked me anything at all about Suslovitch or Russian tactics. He went to meet a superior force without recon, without intelligence, without knowing the enemy.

"There, Carter," he said, pointing. His eyesight was more acute than mine. I had to use my binoculars, now a bit battered and cracked but still serviceable, to see the tiny moving line of Russian guerrillas. "They will wind slowly around that mountain and come through the valley floor under our feet."

I looked down. A relatively level valley floor stretched for miles in either direction. The canyon sides weren't all that tall, compared with other valleys nearby.

"That makes it all the better," I said. "Your snipers can be posted on the cliffs. When the Russian column—"

"We fight in our own way."

"The Russians aren't poorly trained guerrillas. They're disciplined and have a top field commander in charge."

"Kali provides. We shall triumph."

His simple acceptance shocked me. It was as if he'd never been in battle before. With the proper preparation, he had a lovely ambush setup. The Old Man did nothing to deploy his men in the proper ways to successfully fight the Russians. I only guessed at what he really planned. Whatever it was, it meant the deaths of a lot of hapless men.

"Where are their tanks?" I asked.

"They are almost through the Khyber Pass. They do not concern us. Not today."

"Send some of your men to dynamite the walls in the pass. Slow the tanks down until government troops can arrive."

"Kali is the protector of the top of the world. We do not need others to aid us in the defense."

I didn't press the issue. The head of the Russian unit rounded a bend in the canyon almost four miles away. I looked to the Old Man's men for some sign that they psyched themselves for battle. Nothing. They lounged around, some smoking marijuana, others idly polishing gunstocks or honing knives. With their usual taciturnity, they said nothing. With the enemy in sight, they did damn little.

"Give me a rifle. I'm a good enough shot."

"Kali protects," he repeated, standing with arms crossed.

I shifted uneasily from foot to foot, watching the slow advance below. There should have been a hundred snipers on the far cliff, but there were none. The Russians marched along until the main body of troops came even with our position.

Then the thugs attacked. Straight on down the valley. With knives. Screaming and chanting, praising Kali. The hundred rushing forward posed no threat for the Russians. The soldiers unlimbered their rifles and scattered to either side of the valley, taking positions in the rocks. With slow, firing range measured shots, they cut down all those mounting the suicide attack.

"Is this how Kali protects her own? Those men were slaughtered needlessly!"

"Needlessly?" he asked. "No, they died glorious deaths. Kali is pleased with them. Their reincarnated states will be more exalted than this humble one."

A cry of victory went up from the Russians. Then other sounds mixed in. Choking, gurgling, even sloshing noises reaching all the way to the top of the cliff. I trained my binoculars on the Soviet position. I couldn't find a single Russian guerrilla.

"What's going on?" I demanded. "What's happening down there?"

"Come. Let us go and see for ourselves."

The Old Man started down a winding, treacherous path on the face of the cliff. Again, it came to me that he wasn't really old. His nimble steps and sure footing presented a model I was hard-pressed to match. It took fifteen minutes of slipping and sliding to reach the bottom of the rock face, then another five minutes of brisk walking across the valley floor. I had my Luger out and in hand, sure that the clatter of AK-47s would sound at any instant.

Only the wind howling down the valley from the tallest mountains could be heard.

"Here," said the Old Man of the Mountains, nudging a form in deep shadow with his toe.

I went over and examined the corpse. A Russian. His throat had been slit.

"And look over there, as well." He stood, arms crossed, his expression virtually unreadable.

I made a quick circuit through the area, Wilhelmina back in her holster. Every Russian I found was dead, throat slit from ear to ear.

"It is not our way to enter a protracted firefight. Their rifles are heavier. They carry more ammunition. This way is simpler, more effective."

"I don't understand what happened." As I examined the Russians, I noticed that all of the Kali cultists who'd been mowed down by Soviet machine gun fire were gone, as if they had never existed.

"A few select of our group distracted the soldiers. They took cover, broke ranks, directed their attention forward, into the valley. The rest of Kali's force slipped down the mountain face, quietly came up from behind and practiced their ancient arts without fight.''

"But a hundred died!"

"Many times that number might have died in a firefight," said the Old Man. "This is more effective.''

How simple, I thought. Distract the Russians, get their attention focused in one and only one spot, then quietly slip up from behind and practice *thuggee*. Assassinate each and every one. I doubted there were any more casualties on Kali's forces than the initial one hundred in their suicide run.

I didn't know if I admired them or feared them for their fanaticism.

TWENTY-TWO

"Suslovitch wasn't among them? You didn't get their commander?" I felt as if I'd stepped into an elevator and found out the car was already on its way to the basement.

The Old Man said nothing, his face as impassive as if he'd been told it might rain this afternoon.

"Don't you understand? If Suslovitch is not there, another force will be coming. The man's a genius. He won't fall for the same trap these guerrillas fell into. He knows there is powerful opposition to his incursion."

"Kali does not care about whether the enemy knows or not. Kali gives all her followers supreme strength, total confidence. It matters little whether or not the *kafir* leader of the Russians is among the dead. He soon will succumb to Kali's embrace."

"You're talking about another suicide squad," I said angrily, looking out over the scene of the slaughter.

"If it serves our goddess. Why are you so concerned? You act as if those dead were not achieving a state of grace higher than they now have. They are being exalted."

"Westerners have a different view of death," was all I said. The difference struck me hard and kept hitting me when I least expected it. Religions in the West promise immortality in life after death. Eastern religions preach reincarnation until the highest state of grace is attained, then real death.

133

"Are your views of military matters so different, also?" he asked.

"Yes. While the Russians are a curious combination of Asiatic and European, they fight a good deal like Europeans. Arkady Suslovitch will not blindly follow. If he has another gunship, he'll send it in. Throat cutting doesn't work when you're faced with a hovering platform laden with the most devastating weapons possible."

"We die in Kali's cause."

"You die for nothing if the Russians use their poison gas or cannon or rockets on you. There's no way of fighting back. Look at what your men do. They're leaving behind the Russians' weapons. Take them, use them against the Russians. That's what the Sikhs do and that's what the Mujeheddin do in Afghanistan."

"The Mujeheddin are Muslim. The Sikhs are almost so. We scorn the weapons."

The Old Man of the Mountains lifted his chin slightly in defiance. I knew arguing the point wouldn't get me anywhere. He was stubborn and opinionated and, worst of all, he'd been right so far. But the Russians weren't going to keep throwing their men down this valley. They'd scout it completely and provide air support, if they got another gunship over the mountains from their base in Kabul or brought down some from their base in Zebak.

"At least throw the rifles into a deep canyon. Toss the ammo out, too. Keep the Russians from recovering it."

"Do so," the Old Man said to his military commandant. The man spun and went to tell the cultists. Laughing and jeering, they threw all the Russian weapons— and the bodies, too—into deep gullies and over the sides of mountains.

I hurried over as they dragged the bodies of a rocket crew out to heave over into a ravine. I rescued the rocket launcher one of them carried and the rockets another had loaded into a special knapsack on his back.

"Go ahead," I said, waving my hand at the thugs. They smiled, giving me broken-toothed grins, and then enjoyed themselves throwing the barbarians they'd slain in battle over the edge. I felt closer to the Russians than I'd ever felt before. While their goals were wrong and their methods brutal, I understood them. The Kali death cult thugs were aliens to me.

If only I could convince the Old Man that I did know how the Russians reacted in cases like this.

Shaking my head, I lugged the hand-held rocket launcher and rockets up the mountain to where he waited. He'd promised a big celebration tonight. I wondered if there'd be a human sacrifice to Kali.

A willing one.

"The Russians come over from Afghanistan through the other pass, Old Man of the Mountains," reported one of the scouts working north along the Hindu Kush.

"The Manda Pass," he said, nodding. "Near Chitral."

I closed my eyes and tried to visualize the map of the area I'd seen. That was rugged area, really rugged. The pass was almost fifteen thousand feet. The mountains in the Hindu Kush rose up way high around it. But if the Russians got across that pass, they simplified their supply problems. Their airbase at Zebak could furnish all the helicopters they wanted. While impossible to fly a heavily armored chopper across the pass, a turbocharged and stripped down model could make it, then be refitted on the other side.

"Are their gunships coming across?" I asked.

"Many. They darken the skies at times," said the scout.

"Damn," I muttered. Louder, "This is it. Suslovitch's called in the cavalry."

"What?"

"An expression meaning he's got reinforcement coming, reinforcement we can't fight."

"Kali is supreme. We fight. We win."

"Believing it to be true doesn't make it so."

"*Maya*," said the Old Man of the Mountains. "The world is all illusion."

"They're bringing very real death. If they're pushed into a corner, they won't even refit the helicopters. Poison gas doesn't weigh very much. They'll bring enough to gas the entire valley, any valley where your men might be. They don't care about taking life."

"They eat cows," said a man in the back of the crowd gathered around the Old Man's table.

"If you try to fight those helicopters without ground-to-air missiles, you're dead."

"Kali . . ." he began, but was interrupted by a man pushing through the crowd.

"Old Man of the Mountains," said the newcomer. "They send a scouting team into the valley."

I tried to remember what sign of battle had been left. The cultists had been thorough removing the bodies and tossing them down the sides of mountains. While the guerrillas might find their comrades, these were big mountains. They might go on through without stopping.

"Don't try to engage them," I said quickly. "Let them go on. If they report back to Suslovitch that they can't find anything, he might try another expedition."

"No. We kill them, too. This is war."

He meant religious war. A *jihad* as the Moslems would say. No quarter asked or given. Total annihilation. Death to all, and to hell with strategic priorities.

"Suslovitch'll know for sure where his men bought it. Let the scouting party go."

"Our men attack now," said the thug reporting in.

"Good, Hanuman. You have done well."

We silently filed out and went the mile or so to the battle site. The cultists tried the same tactic and found the Russians warier. They didn't allow anyone to sneak up behind them unseen. Their defense perimeter ran a full three hundred and sixty degrees. Even worse than being holed up in the center of the valley was the thin antenna wire extending upward. While the rock walls held in most of the transmission, I didn't have any doubt that Suslovitch had arranged a relay system.

"Are there others in the mouth of the valley?" I asked. A simple nod gave me my answer. The Russians trapped now had reported in, radioing to the group at the valley mouth. They in turn radioed to another unit further back and so on until Suslovitch received his report. It was a modern equivalent of a semaphore system.

"They fight well," said the Old Man. "It does them no good."

From the bodies strewn on the floor of the valley, I wondered who he talked about. One by one the Russians died, but they took ten, a dozen, a score of thugs with them. The carnage was incredible.

"Show me the unit at the entrance to the valley. We'll take them out in a different way."

The Old Man of the Mountains looked at me curiously, then shrugged. "Do as he says," he ordered Hanuman, then turned back to watch the progress below.

I took five men with me, in addition to the smiling Hanuman. We arrived to find the Russians pinned in, groups of cultists above and below them in the valley. The guerrillas warily kept them at bay. I knew all I had to do was to command in the name of Kali and to a man the thugs would attack. For a fleeting instant, I savored that complete power, then pushed it out of my mind. I didn't need power. I needed swift victory to send back as a message to Suslovitch.

"That rock outcropping above them," I said. "Can we get ropes and drop in on them silently, quickly?"

Hanuman ordered ropes brought, pleased at having a command, however small, of his own. I fastened the end of one around a big boulder, then readied myself for a quick rappelling down. If any of the Russians looked up for the few seconds I was in the air, suspended and vulnerable, the game was over for me.

"Have the men down below fake an attack in five minutes," I ordered.

"Fake? How?" Hanuman obviously didn't understand the niceties of war, such as diversionary tactics. He had learned nothing from the Old Man.

"Start in, draw fire, then retreat."

"Retreat?" the thug said, as if unfamiliar with the word. Maybe he was.

"Go back to their original position. Do it!"

"At once!" Hanuman melted away, wondering what kind of fool the Old Man of the Mountains had ordered him to obey. In a few minutes he returned.

"Now," I said, when I saw the slow movement of men down below. The machine guns began barking and lead danced off into the air. I took a quick look down, then stepped into space. As fast as I went down, the cultists descended faster. This was their medium; they knew all there was to know about mountains and rock climbing.

I hit the ground in the middle of the Russian circle and immediately grappled with a sallow, flat-faced Asiatic soldier. I was taller, stronger and outweighed him. Forcing him to the ground, I held my Luger against his temple. The fight went out of him. I had a man, probably a non-com, to interrogate.

Or so I thought.

The single shot struck him directly between the eyes. Blood and brains spattered onto my shirt front in a grisly cascade. I jerked my attention up to see Hanuman standing, smiling. The others had been slaughtered; he had assumed I wanted this one killed, too.

"You fool!" I screamed, launching myself at him. Hanuman backed away, puzzled.

"But you said to get them."

I relaxed a little, but my anger smoldered. Explaining to them that I needed information on Soviet supply lines meant nothing. I spun and stalked off, back down the valley where so much blood had been spilled this day.

TWENTY-THREE

I heard the straining helicopters an hour before dawn. The thugs had pitched camp in an exposed area on the side of the mountain. While it cut off attack from one direction, it also reduced the number of places to hide now that it was necessary.

"Awake, get everybody awake!" I shouted. Already angry murmurs passed through the camp. Getting a full two thousand men stirring on such short notice wasn't going to be easy. "Choppers. Get under cover. Try and knock them down with rifle fire."

The Old Man appeared, giving the impression that he never indulged in such a mortal pursuit as sleep.

"What is it, Carter?"

"Russian gunships. They're going to come in. If they strafe the camp, they'll kill about all of us. They've got rockets, too." I already pulled out my captured rocket launcher and looked around for Hanuman. The man had been fascinated with my description of the way the launcher operated. I'd need him to help me. This was a two-man unit.

"Kali protects us."

"Kali will see you all in shallow graves," I snapped. "Suslovitch isn't fooling around this time. Those choppers are going to be equipped with everything they've got. They may even use poison gas. Holding your breath against a mycotoxin doesn't work, either. It gets in through the skin. You start kicking around on the ground, your nervous system shot. You're aware something's wrong with your body but no command works. You've been cut off; your body's turned traitor."

The Old Man said nothing. A simple wave of his hand sent a ripple through the assembled thousands of thugs. If I hadn't seen it I wouldn't have believed it. They melted away, vanishing as if the rock swallowed them. Maybe it had. There were tunnels and caves in these hills I knew nothing of.

"Are they going to be safe?" I asked. "Against being spotted from the air?"

"The Soviet gunships will not be able to machine gun them down. Kali is gracious."

I said nothing, lugging the rocket launcher with me to an overlook down the valley. Dark, ominous shapes hovered. Floodlights searched restlessly against the terrain. No movement caused reaction from the gunship crews.

"Hanuman!" I called. "Load me. Like I showed you this afternoon." I heard feet scraping on rock. The thug pressed in close. I felt nimble hands working at the pack slung over my shoulder. The load lightened, then shifted to the rocket launcher tube.

I sighted and never hesitated. I'd spotted the telltale nozzles poking out from under one of the copters. This one definitely had the poison gas spraying equipment on it. The lance of fire from the launcher momentarily blinded me. The burst of light as the gunship exploded took away all my night vision.

Behind me, I heard Hanuman praying fervently to Kali.

"Load me!" I ordered. "There's another copter there. Let's try for it, too."

"Let me. Let me blow them up!"

Hanuman refused to obey. Cursing, I passed over the launcher and loaded for him. The launcher had been designed to be used by a semi-literate in the Russian Army. Maybe Hanuman could operate it successfully. I hoped so. I wanted that second chopper knocked down before it got nasty about losing its friend.

I shut my eyes when I saw Hanuman's finger jerk back on the trigger. The rocket went out, wide. It missed the chopper by a considerable distance, but this hardly mattered to the enthusiastic thug. He whooped with glee, as if this were a Fourth of July fireworks display at the football stadium.

"This is great!" he said, laughing. "Again. Let me do it again."

I started to load, then saw what happened in the air. The copter turned slowly, floodlights stabbing into the dark. They found us without any problem.

"Run, Hanuman, run for cover!"

"We fight. Let me fire this again." He sat, wiggling his finger in mock firing on the trigger.

"Come on!" I tugged at his sleeve but he remained where he was. Before I got him on his feet, the concussion of a rocket exploding a few yards away picked me up and casually tossed me over the cliff. Flailing, I felt rock brushing against my fingertips. The outjutting of rock saved me. I landed hard, getting the wind knocked out, but somehow I clung to a rock spire twenty feet under where Hanuman hooted at the Russians.

This time they used their 20mm cannon. His body exploded as if they'd jammed a stock of dynamite into him and lit it.

I waited for a strafing run, but it never came. Regaining my breath, pulling myself up, I saw why. The gunship I'd knocked down billowed yellow gas. The wind whipping down from the high mountains caught the cloud of golden death and strung it in long, greasy fingers through the valley. The helicopter crew didn't take any chances. They wanted to be far away to give the gas time to dissipate.

Scrambling for dear life, I regained the top of the cliff, saw the red smears where Hanuman had stood, then ran like hell.

The concussion, the force of my sudden landing, the gas, all of that worked to drive me temporarily insane. I ran blindly. Only when I smashed into the robed figure of the Old Man did I return to the here and now. I sat down cross-legged before him and simply shook in anger, rage and frustration.

Why couldn't I make him understand? The Russians played a deadly game, one that his primitive methods would never win.

"They come over the mountains in greater numbers. They have partial control of the Manda Pass now."

"They aren't even trying to get materiel through the Khyber Pass?" I asked.

"Yes, there, too."

It all came to me in a haze. The Russians formed a double pincers movement, one to the north at Manda and another at Khyber Pass. The resistance had been too great to trust a single thrust into the heart of the country. I had been too effective; I'd caused them to redouble their efforts. How could I fight against a dual attack aimed at Karachi?

The Sikhs no doubt still held their own, and would until the tanks arrived through the Khyber Pass. But with gunships coming through Manda Pass in ever increasing numbers, the tide would turn against them. I shook my head, feeling as if the insides rattled. I didn't think straight. Why should Suslovitch care about the Sikhs? Why bother attacking there at all? He needed those gunships for Karachi, where Pakistani Army units would oppose him. He'd bypass the Sikhs.

He'd leapfrog all the resistance in the mountains. With the capital under his control, the conquest was almost accomplished. Mopping up operations in the mountains could be done at leisure.

I sank down into a camp chair and felt every ache and pain in my tortured body. Since reaching the Kali worshipers, I'd been hammered, banged on and subjected to the most outrageous humiliations. But I'd won their support.

For all that was worth. I knew now how Pandora had felt. I'd opened up the box, all right, but had gotten out a lot more than I'd bargained for. The Old Man of the Mountains had his own ideas of how to proceed and no amount of talking, cajoling or arguing swayed him. I think he actually believed he was well over three hundred years old. He'd said it enough times that his brain refused to accept anything else as the truth. How can any mere mortal argue with a man that old, who defies reincarnation by not dying, who talks directly to the goddess Kali herself?

"The Russian Colonel Suslovitch is assembling forces here and here," he said. I forced my attention back to the map. Arkady Suslovitch had gotten his troops ready at the mouth of the Khyber Pass. "The tanks finish rolling through in two days, perhaps less."

"How many men do you command?" I asked.

"Half a million," came the answer. For a moment, I thought he was joking. No hint of amusement showed.

"Half a million?" I said weakly.

"We will meet these metal forts," he said casually. "Kali will provide."

"That many might slow them down," I admitted. "But what about the gunships coming through the Manda Pass?"

"We split the force."

I thought of the entire plains in front of the Khyber Pass filling with screaming cultists, all waving knives, praying to Kali. That had to stop Suslovitch in his tracks. But what of the gunships? I had an idea about that, too, one I hardly wanted to consider but had to.

"No, don't split your forces. Stop those tanks." He nodded curtly. "And assign me a few of your men to go through the Manda Pass and into Afghanistan."

"Why?"

"I want to knock out the supply center at Zebak, about here." I pointed out the city's location nestled in the middle of the Hindu Kush. The altitudes around here were high. There they were stratospheric. Such an expedition had to be done quickly, without any fuss, with lightning sureness. We had to operate as a strike team, getting in undetected, doing our job, then making like a bat out of hell. The chances of surviving weren't exceptionally good, but even partial success spelled the end of the Kremlin's adventure.

Kali could count the tanks stopped. I'd stop the gunships to the north. The cultists dying as martyrs might be able to jump a step or two in their reincarnation; they'd certainly please Kali herself. The best I hoped for personally was not dying too messy a death.

It wasn't something I looked forward to, but it was what I'd been sent to do: stop the Russians.

TWENTY-FOUR

"Nick, don't go," pleaded Ananda. "You will only die. Let the Mujeheddin do what they can against the Russian soldiers. That is their country."

"Afghanistan's theirs," I said, holding her at arm's length, "but the Russians aren't content with staying north across the border and fighting only the Mujeheddin. They're making their big move now—and it's heavily backed. If I can knock out the Soviet air base at Zebak, it cuts one leg out from under Suslovitch's assault."

"And the followers of Kali hack at the other leg," said Gupta Dasai. Both he and his sister had remained in the city under the mountain. Only when word of the helicopter attack came did they insist on emerging. I knew what Ananda's motive for leaving the safety of the city was. I had no idea about Dasai's.

"That's it. If only the Pakistani government would come to their senses. It's as if a war is being fought under their noses and they don't know it."

"They might not. This is rugged country. Radio contact with the rest of Pakistan is minimal," said Ananda.

"True, but there ought to be government posts throughout the region. Certainly along the border. They shouldn't allow the Shinwari to maintain all trade through the Khyber Pass."

"The Shinwari have been loyal to the Pakistani government prior to this," said the woman. "And never before has the rule of Kali been challenged in these hills."

"Things are coming loose all around," I said. Heaving a deep sigh, I told the woman, "I've got to go try. It's my job."

"Your karma," she said softly.

"However you want to call it."

"I am going, also."

For a moment, I thought Ananda had spoken. But her lips only quivered slightly, holding back the words neither of us wanted spoken. This wasn't the time or place to talk of love. Then I realized it had been her brother who said he was accompanying me.

"You can't, Gupta," I told him. "This is going to be a quick march, through the pass at fifteen thousand feet, then a strike into Afghanistan. It's possible none of us will survive it. Stay here. Take care of your sister."

The look he gave me held more than simple words can relate. I read the horror he had lived through, the loss he suffered, the ways he had been made into something less than a man. According to his code, he had failed repeatedly. What that did to his next reincarnation, I had no idea, but it wasn't good. He silently begged me for the chance to recover some of his lost honor by making the grand gesture, the big play.

I didn't want him tagging along, but I understood what he was going through.

"We leave in ten minutes," I said to him. He nodded and went to assemble a pack.

"You shouldn't have done that, Nick," said Ananda.

"He would have followed. Better that we work together. He's a good man. Conditions have been more than he can handle or cope with. Maybe this . . . mission is what he needs." I had started to say suicide mission, but that didn't seem too prudent. Ananda already risked the last two men in her life that meant anything to her. No need to drive home the point even more.

"You are right. Take care of him, Nick." She stood on tiptoe and quickly kissed me, then turned and ran. I started to call out to her, to stop her, then knew it wouldn't do either of us any good.

Dasai, five Kali cultists and I hit the trail to Manda Pass immediately.

I was glad to have the thugs along. They knew the easiest trails—easy being a relative term—and we made incredibly quick progress. Before nightfall we looked down at the pass and the Soviet column moving through it.

"They're shipping a lot of equipment on trucks," I said. "Probably the fittings for the gunships. They strip the copters down, fly them through, then refit on this side."

"How do we get past the guards?" asked Dasai. He had spotted the Russian sentries patrolling the mouth of the pass.

I started to say I hadn't the foggiest idea, when all of a sudden I knew. Everything fit together perfectly. Glancing at the five thugs, I wondered if it would work. Everything depended on their training, how well they obeyed orders. Then I remembered the frontal assault on the Russian position. Those hundred had died for their goddess because the Old Man of the Mountains had ordered them to. There'd be no trouble now.

There couldn't be.

I quickly outlined my plan.

The dense night was relieved only by the brilliance of the stars. They looked as if I could reach out and touch them. I tried to keep my mind off the skirmish ahead by working through the names of the stars, their designations; then I heard Dasai clear his throat.

We were ready to go.

Kali's thugs moved as softly as shadows. I drifted behind them, equally as silent. Only Dasai had trouble. To my ears it seemed he herded elephants, but it didn't matter. We found the Russian guards dozing. Hugo drank deeply of the first soldier's blood. Knives backed by Kali's bloodthirsty might eliminated the others quickly. The entire battle had lasted only seconds.

"Get them out of their uniforms. Quickly, before you get blood on them."

We stripped the soldiers of their uniforms, spent a few minutes trying to get everyone into the best fit. I had to take the sergeant's jacket, even though it stretched much too tight across my shoulders. I was the only one of the group who spoke Russian.

"Into the truck," I ordered. Dasai checked the fuel and made certain that our five friends in the back knew they were to keep their kill-frenzy under control and to not utter a word. They might die back there, but I wanted it to be without a fight. We either got through without a hitch or no amount of fighting would save us.

I worried the engine until it finally, reluctantly started. Switching on the headlights, I turned the truck back through the Manda Pass and drove for Afghanistan.

Getting through the checkpoint was easier than I'd anticipated. The constant stream of men and materiel coming through confused everyone. Paperwork ran hours or days behind actual shipments.

"Where are you going?" demanded the guard.

"Back to Zebak," I said in Russian. "Orders are not to wait for daylight."

"Whose orders?"

"Comrade, are you telling me to stay here, to get a good night's sleep, maybe find hot food, drink a bottle of vodka, rather than drive into this asshole-dark canyon filled with guerrillas shooting at me? If you are telling me that, I thank you."

"Go on," the guard said, signaling that the gate be raised.

"Too bad," I said. He waved me on. I gunned it.

The drive through the pass took most of the night. By the hour before dawn, we pulled up outside the Soviet airbase at Zebak, miles inside Afghanistan.

"What now?" asked Dasai, glancing at the thugs. "Those in the back are getting restless."

I heard the five honing their knives, checking side-arms captured from the dead Russians. They were ready to fight for their goddess. I wasn't quite as sure how to use them. The airbase looked primitive in comparison to many of the Soviet installations I've seen around the world. The landing strip was long, very long, but there was only one. The length was necessary because of the high altitude. The thin air reduced lift and required much longer takeoffs. The heavy cargo planes bringing in the helicopter gunships might require over two miles to brake, due to their heavy loads, too.

It didn't appear likely I could do much damage to the runway itself. On the other hand, the one thing both choppers and cargo planes had in common was a need for fuel.

"The fuel dump," I said. "Let's find it. Tell the boys in the back to keep their mouths shut. Until I give the word." When the word might be needed, I had no idea. Up to that point, I didn't want them upsetting the apple cart with an ill-chosen word in praise of Kali or taking offense and killing the wrong guard.

We drove to the main gate, got in line and waited. The number of trucks entering the air base worried me. While there was safety in numbers and the chances of getting inside increased, so much activity meant Suslovitch's offensive might be under way.

"Come for another load of ammo?" the guard at the gate asked, checking our truck number. I thanked the high mountains between India and Afghanistan for blocking out most radio transmission. Even if the Russians had found the driver and the others dead and their truck missing on the Indian side, only a messenger driving through the pass could bring that information to this side.

"All ready," I said in my best Russian.

The guard looked up, frowned. "I do not recognize you."

"New driver," I said quickly. "The Mujeheddin got the last one. Ambush just this side of the pass, from what I hear."

"Another, eh?" he said, shaking his head. The resignation in his voice cheered me. The Afghanistan Mujeheddin did a good job of keeping the Soviets on their toes. "Go on. I'm glad I'm not ferrying ammunition in this country."

I drove into the base, then had to stop. A real driver knew where the ammo dump was; I didn't. Another truck pulled up beside us, the man beside the driver shouting, "What's wrong?"

"Engine trouble. Altitude. Vapor lock," I said. "You going to the ammo dump?"

"We are."

"I'll follow and honk if there is any more trouble."

The Russians waved and started off. I followed at a slower clip, letting them get well ahead. On the way, I saw my real target. The fuel tanks for the cargo planes as well as the helicopter gunships were partially buried near the control tower. Take out the tanks and the control crew went up, too. Neat. All I needed was the stuff to make the boom.

"Get ready," I called back to the cultists. I heard hammers cocking on pistols and the snick of steel against sheath as razor-sharp deadly knives came out. Pulling up next to the other truck, its crew already loading boxes of machine gun ammo into the back, I shouted, "Now! For Kali!"

The eruption of sudden death from the back of my truck took the Russians by storm. Four lay dead, their throats cut, before they even realized anything was wrong. I used my Luger to good advantage, taking out two guards who had partially unlimbered their rifles. The rest was easy—until one of the Russians managed to pull himself to the door of the ammo dump and drag himself inside.

"Stop him!" I yelled.

Dasai was closest. He fired a rifle he'd picked up. The Russian jerked as the heavy slugs ripped into his body, making him dance like a rag doll in a windstorm, but the effort came too late. The soldier slammed shut the door. I heard the heavy bar drop inside.

We were locked out.

I took a quick head count. Of Kali's five best, only two remained. With Dasai and me, that made four remaining to complete the mission. But already I heard sirens shrieking out their alarm. The gunfire had been overheard in the still dawn. What little time we had evaporated all too quickly to suit me.

"No time for finesse," I said, jumping into the truck and revving the engine. "Get back. Cover me." Slamming the heavy vehicle into gear, it bucked forward as I popped the clutch. The front fender smashed through the door to the ammo dump.

"Hurry," Dasai cried, motioning to the remaining thugs. "Load the explosives."

"Look out!" I swung around the door frame, Luger in hand. I fired, an instant too late. The Russian who had taken refuge inside the dump managed to fire once, hitting Gupta Dasai in the middle of the back. The man dropped like he'd been sandbagged. My shot took the top off the Russian soldier's head, forming a bloody pool on the floor. The two thugs didn't appear to even notice as they kicked their way in past the splintered door and hunted for the explosives. They lived with violent death on a day to day basis; for that matter, so did I, but they'd become used to it. I never had.

"Dasai, are you all right?" I cradled his head.

"Destroy the fuel tanks," he said. "I am all right." He lied. I felt the sticky wetness spreading across my hands and legs where I held him.

"Here goes," I said, heaving him up and onto my shoulders. Moving him like this might kill him; leaving him behind meant sure death. I put him in the front seat of the second truck. His pallor alarmed me, but I didn't have an instant to spare. Already I heard tanks coming to life. In a few minutes, the entire air base would be awake and deadly.

"There, those, get that," I said, pointing, moving through the bunker. The two Kali worshipers gave me wolfish grins and loaded what I said. When fully half the back of the truck had been packed with high explosive, I let them keep on with the muscle work while I rigged a couple of detonators. One was a straight timer. I set it for ten minutes. The other was a deadman's switch: release the button and everything went up. No matter what happened, this truck was going to go.

"What is this?" asked one of the thugs, eyeing my haphazard wiring. I glanced up and a cold shiver went down my spine. He asked what I did, but the look on his face told me he understood everything perfectly.

"Release this button and everything goes up," I said, not mentioning the ten minute timer, already started and silently ticking. "I've got to wire this up."

"Here?" he asked, pointing.

"Right."

"For Kali!" he screamed, shoving me back. I slipped and fell heavily, hitting my head against the second truck's frame. For a moment, stars spun and blackness crept in. I held on and struggled back to my feet. By the time my eyes focused again, the truck roared across the tarmac, directly for the fuel tanks.

The man released the dead man's switch at exactly the proper instant to cause the most damage. I should have known that one of the thugs couldn't pass up the opportunity to die for his goddess; the ten minute timer had been a waste of effort. Along with the explosion and roar of igniting airplane fuel, I heard one last, *"Kali!"*

I wiped at the bloody spot on my scalp and decided I'd live—unless I just stood around. Jumping into the truck, I got it running and drove for the far end of the field, away from the blazing tanks. Beside me, Dasai moaned softly, the blood seeping out to stain the vinyl seat-covers. Getting him back into Pakistan wasn't going to be simple. Getting him back alive presented even bigger problems.

Braking, I screeched to a halt ten feet from where the props of a large gunship kicked up dust.

"Wait!" I shouted in my most commanding tone. Russian has certain cases to use that don't exist in English. I made full use of them to sound like an officer used to being obeyed. It worked. The door of the chopper opened and the flight master jumped out to see what was wrong.

"In the cab. Wounded general," I shouted over the copter's roar. The non-com's eyes went wide at the thought of a Russian general being injured. I had no doubt he knew of General Shkidschenko's death, even if it wasn't officially declared.

"But he isn't—" the flight master started, seeing Dasai's uniform markings.

"Get him into the gunship," I said. My voice dripped Siberian ice. The man jumped to obey. And I jumped to shove him out and slam the door in his face once Dasai was safely aboard.

A quick shot from my Luger took out the pilot and I slipped into the copilot's seat, not bothering to get rid of the corpse riding beside me. The controls were similar to those I'd seen in other choppers. It took only seconds to lift off and avoid the flight master's questing fingers. Then we were airborne.

I turned toward Manda Pass, wondering if I could negotiate the high-walled canyons in a copter that strained just to stay in the air at this altitude. One look back at Dasai told me I didn't have any choice. I speeded up the rotors and headed into the pass.

TWENTY-FIVE

The helicopter blades whined less than an inch from the stone walls as I navigated through the canyon. At other times, the wheels brushed the rocky ground, shaking the craft and making control hazardous at best. I was drenched in nervous perspiration by the time I came out the far side of the pass and glad to see open spaces larger than the width of the gunship. The chopper had sucked up gas like it had a hole in the tank and, even more obnoxious, the body beside me had passed through rigor mortis and was beginning to decay. It felt like an eternity flying through the pass, but it had only been a matter of hours.

For the first time since beginning the treacherous flight, I had a chance to look back at Gupta Dasai. He lay where I'd dropped him. A puddle of his own blood had formed, but it hadn't spread to the point where it panicked me. I caught sight of shallow movement in his chest. He still breathed. Gupta Dasai was a lot tougher than even I had given him credit for.

The radio crackled and whined. The incoming call was from another Soviet copter operating on this side of the pass. I kept on my course, ignoring the message, until the other ship matched my course, not fifty feet away. I pointed to the dead pilot and made motions like the Mujeheddin had done us in. The other pilot wanted me to land, thinking that my radio had been shot out of commission, too.

Landing was the last thing in the world I wanted to do, but the sight of the gunner hanging on his heavy machine gun in the open doorway of the other helicopter decided me. I set down and spun around a little, to give myself a fighting chance.

I quickly got out of the copilot's seat and dived for the back of the copter. Checking the heavy machine gun suspended near the hatch, I jacked in a round, then pushed open the door. There wasn't a second to waste. I gave them no quarter, the heavy 12mm slugs ripping apart crew chief, pilot, copter. I fired until my shoulders ached, then leaned on the firing lever some more. It took me long seconds to realize that I'd run out of ammo. The belt had been exhausted and lay in an empty tangle on the far side of my gun.

"Carter," came Dasai's weak voice. "Are we . . ."

"We're back on the Indian side of the border," I told him. "Hang in there. We'll meet up with the Old Man of the Mountains again and get some medical attention for you."

"We did well?" he asked. I knew what he wanted me to say, so I said it.

"You're a hero, Gupta. Without you, this mission would have failed. You're not a soldier and I can't promise you a medal, but I swear you won't be forgotten. The U.S. never forgets an ally."

He smiled and settled back, his face as white as a ghost. But he was content. If he died now, he died knowing that his life wasn't a lie, that he had accomplished something in the face of extreme adversity. Even more, his act might have saved his country from a foreign aggressor.

I started back up to the cockpit when I heard rock banging against rock. Turning, hand on pistol, I froze. A dozen rifles pointed at me through the door.

"Kali!" I shouted. For a moment, no one moved. Then the man in front smiled.

"*Kali*!" he shouted back.

The Old Man's thugs had found us.

* * *

"They move in force now," said the Old Man of the Mountains, indicating the path taken by the Russian forces. I sat and simply stared. I needed sleep. The map folded and blurred before me. I had to force myself back to the present, to avoid going into a stupor. Getting Dasai cared for had required a major exertion on my part. The cultists wanted to let him die.

For once, I thought they might have been right. He'd taken a slug almost directly in the middle of his back. While I thought his spine was still intact, the damage down to his ribs and the organs inside had to be massive. He needed a doctor and an intensive care unit in a modern hospital. It might have been kinder to let him die, since those things were out of the question.

When I saw the expression on Ananda's face, I knew Dasai had to be saved. I'd insisted and the members of the *lashkar* war party had finally agreed.

"The tanks have been held up with explosives along their path."

"How long before they dig through?" Like the U.S. military, the Soviets never sent only a tank unit. Along with it went a heavy construction team, with earthmovers and other equipment designed to smooth the way.

"Another day," The Old Man said, shrugging. "The explosives were old, did not work well. Also, the Russians show great ambition in reaching the Pakistani side of the pass."

"What about here at Manda Pass? Are they still ferrying equipment through?"

"Only by truck. Their flying machines come no more. You stopped them?"

"Must have," I admitted. Without flight fuel, that grounded their gunships. The destruction to the base at Zebak wasn't easily repaired, either. Not only had the fuel tanks been taken out, but the control tower with all its valuable communications gear, as well. It took time to replace the electronics needed to land heavily laden cargo planes. Replacing the controllers might be a problem, too. If they took experienced men from Kabul's military airport, that meant the push through the Khyber Pass wasn't properly supplied with incoming materiel. Sealing up Zebak had eliminated the second pincers movement Arkady Suslovitch had intended on using to force Pakistan to her knees.

Now all I had to worry about was the tank force caught in the Khyber Pass. Once it came through, Suslovitch hardly needed air support.

"Nick," said Ananda, concern in her voice. "You wobble about like a child's top. Are you injured?"

"Tired," I said. "Been through too much."

"You should sleep."

"Can't. Gotta help the Old Man. Colonel Suslovitch isn't resting. Son of a bitch is plotting."

I was asleep in her arms even as the words came out.

"There must be five hundred!" I exclaimed. From a hill overlooking the plains facing the Khyber Pass I saw the Russian encampment. Suslovitch had been reinforced until he was well past company strength. With tank support and a reliable supply line behind him reaching through to Kabul, there was little to stop him.

I'm sure that our State Department had men and women arguing themselves blue in the face trying to convince the powers that be that the Russians were, indeed, capable of such a major breach of international law.

This constituted an act of war, nothing less.

I knew that even photographs might not convince the Pakistani officials. Photos can be faked, retouched. The CIA has done that very thing in the past, to the point that many leaders refuse to believe what is actual in favor of what they hope is reality.

"There are so few of them," said the Old Man of the Mountains, almost wistfully. "It is not like in the old days when the British swarmed all over the Khyber Pass. They held Fort Jamrud. I personally led the charge that took the fort. Brave men, the British. But I do not understand them."

I looked at the white-haired, robed figure standing

with arms crossed. The wind whipped past his leathery face. In the afternoon sunlight he looked like an East Indian equivalent of a cigar store Indian. Chipped from wood, immobile, eyes far-focused, the Old Man of the Mountains represented a breed that had died out generations ago. His world revolved around belief, absolute, total, fanatical belief. It seemed cruel to tell him the world had changed from that of Kali's heyday. Or had it? Was there any difference that the Russians entered other countries, determined to achieve their own obsession-dictated goals? Kali had been a cruel goddess; was the Soviet adventurism any less cruel, both to the citizens of the Soviet Union or her neighbors?

I had a sudden insight that the Old Man might understand the Russians better than anyone else, certainly better than me.

"These men are highly trained and well armed," I said. "Their machine guns kill a hundred times faster than the British rifles did."

"The metal forts, the tanks, they are even more powerful." The way he said it turned the statement into a question, yet I knew he'd seen the awesome firepower of a tank turned against a band of his men as they dynamited the walls in the Khyber Pass.

"Much more powerful," I assured him.

"It will be a good battle," he said, with some satisfaction.

I doubted any battle was a good one.

The first of the Soviet tanks rumbled from the mouth of the pass.

TWENTY-SIX

"You can't use a frontal assault," I said, my voice almost cracking with the strain. "That tank will blow your men to bits before they charge halfway across the plain."

The Old Man of the Mountains studied the positioning of the tank, then nodded, saying, "You are right. We must use a diversion to get close to it."

"Then what?"

"We destroy it. Kali is the goddess of destruction, as well as of birth. Her many aspects serve us well."

"You can't destroy a T-4 tank by wishing it to melt. You have to use something more powerful."

"We have dynamite left."

I cringed. That was almost worse than nothing at all. The explosive had to be forty years old. I'd watched several of the thugs blow themselves up with the unstable dynamite. The sticks sweated, beads of nitro dotting the red sheaths. The blasting caps had hardly been necessary when a good jolt set off case after case. Even the blasting caps themselves had seen finer days. The Russians didn't even need their tank with such fragile, dangerous explosive available to their enemies. All they had to do was sit back and watch the fun.

"The dynamite is little good against the metal," I said. "If you can find rockets, such as the ground-to-air units the Sikhs used. Or the one I used against the Soviets—that Hanuman died using."

"Useless," said the Old Man firmly. "The ancient ways of Kali are best. We will prevail. The goddess herself will come down from her throne to aid her faithful."

"Your men are doing a great job keeping the Russians contained to the valley," I said, trying to change the tact and get something positive accomplished. I wished for a radio capable of contacting the AXE satellite. If I could get through to Hawk, I was positive some sort of anti-tank weapon could be air-dropped in, Pakistani air force be damned. If anything, the Pakistani jets chasing a drop plane might be beneficial if they saw what went on at their back door.

But the Old Man scorned radios. He had personally overseen the destruction of every single one that had fallen into the cultists' hands. He claimed they were unbelievers' tools. I had tried to go back to the gunship Dasai and I had escaped from Afghanistan in, but the Russians had used incendiary rockets on it, totally destroying it rather than let anyone else scavenge parts.

We truly fought a modern guerrilla war. I just wished those in the death cult had better armament. Faith was fine but it let through a lot of very deadly bullets.

"The battle begins soon," he said with some satisfaction. The white-haired man turned and went to talk with his advisors. I wondered about him. He understood that any sort of frontal assault on the tank was suicidal, yet it didn't bother him. The Old Man didn't care if hundreds, or even thousands, of his cult died in futile attacks.

Or maybe he did care and showed it in ways I didn't recognize. I don't know. I wanted to stop the senseless slaughter by a little common sense and knowledge of how the Russians fought and he wouldn't listen. That was the only fact I had to work on.

"Nick," came Ananda's soft voice.

"How's your brother?"

"No better, but he is not slipping away, either. Was . . . was he truly brave in Afghanistan?"

"Yes." I didn't bother qualifying it. There was no need since I told the simple truth.

"I am glad. For his sake. He needed to prove much to himself."

She looked out over the valley. I read in her eyes that she saw the horror to come.

"They're going to be cut down until the bodies are a dozen deep," I said.

"Please, Nick," she said, a tremor in her voice. "It is so senseless."

"That's your Western education talking. What's death?" I said, my tone more bitter than I intended. "Just an opportunity for a new reincarnation, maybe with better chances of making it off the death and rebirth carousel."

"Will he not listen to you?"

"No. And I'll give you a preview of what's to come. Kali is going to watch a bloodbath such as this province hasn't seen in years, maybe centuries." I wanted her to try talking with the Old Man, though I knew that he wouldn't listen to Ananda either. He listened to no woman, except perhaps Kali herself.

"They start."

I watched as a column of cultists moved quickly down into the valley. The Russians didn't immediately open fire. They'd wait, perhaps until all the followers of Kali committed themselves. I wondered at their training, however. It took more than simple courage to face what advanced on them now. Screaming, chanting, a solid wave of humanity rushed forward. Less than a thousand yards from the Soviet encampment, the thugs began a ululating chant that made the hairs on the back of my neck stand up. It was a disconcerting cry, one designed to drive out any bravery in the enemy.

I was glad I didn't face that horde of knife-waving fanatics.

When they were five hundred yards from the tanks, an order passed through the Soviet line. Machine guns opened up and the tank began belching out round after round of exploding steel death.

I turned, not able to look. Still I heard the chant, "*Kali*! *Kali*! *Kali*!" When I looked again, blood ran in rivers down the small gulleys. A new mountain of corpses rose to challenge the Hindu Kush. And surprisingly, the thugs had overrun the first Soviet line, more by sheer numbers and determination than anything else.

"They'll make it," I said in awe, seeing it but not fully believing yet. "The Russians will retreat."

"But they can beat them back, if they stay," protested Ananda.

"No, look. Watch. Colonel Suslovitch will order a retreat. The tanks will give covering fire and his guerrillas will drop back and retrench." Even as I spoke, the Soviets began falling back, one unit retreating while the others on either side gave them covering automatic weapons fire. "They don't fight pitched battles. They prefer to take their losses, regroup, then try again. It's either immediate victory or retreat for them. The Old Man has pushed them back into the mouth of the Khyber Pass!"

I knew that victory was short lived. While the Old Man sent in fresh shock troops for a renewed assault on the new Soviet position, other tanks made their way through the Khyber Pass. Tiny pockets of fighting still existed across the broad plain. At great cost, the cultists wiped out each and every guerrilla unit. I did a quick tally and came to the conclusion that it took twenty of Kali's most faithful to remove one Russian guerrilla. A lousy ratio, even when the Old Man talked of putting a half million thugs into the field.

"They withdrew," said Ananda, a mixture of emotion playing on her face. She was grateful for the respite in the battle, but she also wanted it done with.

Kali's warriors retreated about a mile to allow fresh men and supplies to come forward. They ate, meditated and prepared for another frontal assault on the new Soviet position. Their entire attitude was one of a day's work being done. That bothered me; killing was serious work and deserved more emotional involvement between battles. I studied how Suslovitch grouped, then grabbed for my battered binoculars to see if my eyes deceived me.

"He's got regular Army units with him. Those Russian officers are in field uniform." Suslovitch had dropped all pretense that this was merely a guerrilla band. Red Army companies had been sent through the pass to support his "guerrillas."

"Does this mean that they are totally committed to pushing through to Karachi?"

"I'm afraid so. As long as Suslovitch's men wore guerrilla outfits and didn't show any Soviet Army insignia, they could always back out and lie, saying this was a dissent radical Indian faction or even one of the Mujeheddin groups intending to cause friction between Russia and India. They can't do that now, not with uniformed Russian troops openly fighting."

The next round of battle was joined. This time, both sides reinforced and ready, the slaughter was even more extreme. The Old Man lost forty or more men for every Russian killed. The tanks, the regular Red Army units, their superior arms kept the cultists at bay. When it became obvious to the Old Man of the Mountains that further attack was futile, he recalled his men.

I tried to do a field count of the dead and wounded, using techniques developed at the War College. The Russians might have lost as many as three hundred men, twice that wounded. Kali lost almost ten thousand worshipers, without any significant number wounded. They either fought and died, or they kept fighting.

The Russian position was stronger than ever at the mouth of the Khyber Pass. The only way to attack was either a sneak-up from behind, which wasn't possible with traversing twenty-seven miles of steep canyon from the Afghanistan side, or climbing in mountains even more treacherous. Supplies filtered through the pass from the other side and modern armaments outweighed any numerical advantage the Hindus might have.

By being cautious, Arkady Suslovitch had given the Soviet Union a solid base in Pakistan. Expanding from this point was a matter of supply alone. His big thrust into the heartland wasn't far behind.

Unless Nick Carter, Killmaster, did something about it.

TWENTY-SEVEN

The stars shone down on me, tiny diamond-hard points of spies in the sky. I pulled my coat around me more firmly to keep in my body heat and to block out the high wind whipping off the mountains, then checked the equipment I took with me. It was little enough for a major assault on a fortified Russian position.

Hugo and Wilhelmina went, of course. They were faithful, reliable and had never let me down when I needed them most. The only other weapon I took was a captured AK-47. I don't like the blunderbusses very much, but there were advantages to carrying one tonight. Ready supplies of ammo were available off the ground from fallen soldiers; the distinctive sound might be confused by the Russians for their own men firing and—it was the best weapon available. I didn't want to lug along the Afridi copies of the Lee-Enfields or the Martini-Henrys.

I hadn't told Ananda I was going on a single-man mission behind enemy lines. She wouldn't have understood and I thought she had enough worries with her brother. Gupta Dasai had fallen into a coma from his injuries. I saw that infection had set in. He'd be dead in a very short time unless he was tended by a real doctor with an ample supply of antibiotics. It was hard for me to believe this was the way war used to be fought, with more death from infection than enemy action. The world had changed markedly in the last forty years.

"You go now?" asked the Old Man.

I hadn't told him of my plans, either, but he seemed to know instinctively what I had to do.

"Yes. It'll take about an hour reaching the Russian defense perimeters, then another two for me to get through. I want to get to Suslovitch before dawn."

"Our cult is renowned for assassination," he said, in an offhanded tone. "We can get a thousand assassins in."

"I know that," I said. "This is something I have to do myself." Trying to sort out my real motives for this suicide mission wasn't easy. I wanted Arkady Suslovitch for myself, yes, but it went deeper. The death cult members might have been better trained for murder. I didn't know; I doubted it. They were too deeply mired in the traditions of past centuries to comprehend motion sensors, sonic detectors and other gadgets the Russians might use in the field. I knew; I could get through.

Also, there's the matter of seeing a job done personally. Reports might come back that the Old Man's crack team of assassins had succeeded in killing Suslovitch. A doubt would always remain that they had somehow failed, that the colonel had tricked them or managed to live through the cultists' ignorance. If I killed Suslovitch, I knew he'd be dead, dead, dead.

Or there might be an even better use for him alive, if I played this right.

Most of all I wanted to get behind Russian lines and find one of their radios. A single call to Hawk would get things straightened out in a hurry. He could then supply the State Department with the information that uniformed Russian troops had invaded Pakistan. World press picking it up meant the Pakistanis could no longer ignore what happened on their doorstep. Nor could the Soviets remain on foreign soil. The Kremlin would have to order a pullback.

One lousy radio call. I heaved my captured rifle onto my shoulder, looked back at Ananda, then started off, down the side of the mountain. The rocky trail proved dangerous in the dark and it slowed my progress considerably. I made up for the time lost by dogtrotting across the plains, occasionally slipping in wet spots. Since it hadn't rained, the wetness had to be human blood. The sharp coppery tang in the air only reinforced that image.

"What time is it?" I heard one Russian ask another. I dropped to my belly and worked forward. Suslovitch had established his outer defense points further from the mouth of the pass than I'd anticipated. He didn't want to give Kali's faithful any more lead time to reach his main camp than necessary.

"Nearly midnight," came the answer. I used their voices to pinpoint where the sentries stood. Hugo took out the first. I dropped the carrying strap of my AK-47 around the other's neck and strangled him. A quick search failed to reveal even a field walkie-talkie. I moved on, toward the Khyber Pass.

Men walked patrol while others worked feverishly on their equipment. I'd wondered why the tank barrages hadn't been sustained after the thugs had pulled back. Now I knew. One tank cannon had gotten a shell jammed in the breach mechanism. The other, just arrived, had broken a cogwheel coming through the rocky pass. But by daylight both tanks would be operational and Suslovitch would again be on the offensive.

I moved like a ghost through the guards, hunting for the command tent where Arkady Suslovitch no doubt sat up working on his strategy for the coming day. I found the tent easily enough. It stood to one side and had continual patrols around it.

A problem. But not one that proved insurmountable.

I hid in shadow, waiting. When a sentry about my size came by, I took him out with the butt of my rifle. The darkness was so complete I had to feel rather than see the damage I'd done to him. He had died almost instantly from a crushed skull. I stripped off his uniform and put it on over my clothes. This gave a bulky feel not to my liking, but time pressed. I had to make a move soon. Less than three hours remained before dawn.

Walking a sentry post of my own devising, I heard

Suslovitch's voice inside the tent.

". . . another tank by mid-afternoon. Then we push through these savages and drive directly for New Delhi. The government will collapse in less than a week."

"You are so sure, Colonel?" I didn't recognize the voice but the tone indicated the speaker was KGB. It had an arrogance, a complete assurance of power to it marking the highest ranking field agents.

"Assure me of the supplies needed to support a column between here and Karachi, and then we'll make it *our* capital."

"The savages slow you down. Your timetable is already out of date. You meant to be knocking on the Indians' door by now."

"The Mujeheddin took out the airbase at Zebak. That was beyond my control. Without the gunships being supplied through Manda Pass, I had little other choice but to wait for the tanks to arrive. Even then, the fuel situation is touchy. These Hindus attacking are fanatical. No air support meant I had to consolidate this position. Otherwise, I would be in total control of the country."

"You think so little of their army?" Both men laughed harshly. I nervously fingered my rifle, considering options, making new plans. The radio had been housed in a tent not fifty feet away. I had the feeling I might achieve only one of my two goals. Did I want Suslovitch or a radio message out to Hawk? Either, or, and not both.

I went for Arkady Suslovitch.

"Colonel, a message," I said, staying just outside the tent so that he couldn't see me.

"Let it wait," he said impatiently. "I am busy."

"It is from General Golony."

"Who?"

I'd named an officer high in the GRU, the Russian Military Intelligence, and one I'm sure Suslovitch had once worked under. The KGB and GRU have a continuing fight for internal dominance; if I mentioned the name of a high ranking GRU officer in front of a

KGB officer, sparks had to fly. Suslovitch also had to
see what was in the wind.

"Golony, sir," I repeated for him. "He is in Kabul."

I felt the tension mount in the tent. It broke when
Suslovitch pushed his way out and headed for the radio,
without so much as glancing at me. This might work out
better than I thought; I saw a way to kill two birds with
one stone.

"Stay here," the Russian colonel snapped as the KGB
officer started to follow.

I trailed along, entering the radio tent on Suslovitch's
heels. As the radioman looked up, his eyes widened
slightly at the sight of his commander. When Dmitri saw
me, his mouth gaped. I shoved past Arkady Suslovitch
and slugged the man.

"What?" Suslovitch already went for the Tokarov automatic holstered at his side. The leather flap prevented
a quick draw. I held the AK-47 so that he got the full
benefit of looking down the huge bore.

"So, agent N3," he said, relaxing and letting his hand
fall away from the holster. "We meet again. I am sorry I
missed you the last time, in Hungary. It will not happen
that way again."

"Don't hold your breath, Suslovitch. Turn around." I
pulled his automatic from the holster and stuck it into
my belt. "I've got a bit of radio work to do, but stick
around. I'd hate for you to wander off before inter-
mission."

I spun the dials, found the frequency and began
transmitting without waiting for acknowledgement.
There wasn't time to go through the recognition signal
and counter signal routine. I sent my authorization, the
pertinent facts and let it go at that. If Hawk got the
message, then my authorization sufficed. If not, I'd
saved a little time.

"Now we leave, Colonel," I said.

"Carter, you are a fool if you think I will simply walk
out of here with you. Kill me. It is better than allowing
you to capture me."

"You don't understand, do you, Suslovitch?" I said,

my mind racing. He was right. Getting him out through his own lines might be impossible without his cooperation. "They know."

"'They!'" he asked, arching one eyebrow. "And who is that?"

"The KGB. They know you're defecting. I made sure. It's planted in all the right spots. Three of them, leaked separately in different places around the world."

"No one will believe that."

"The KGB would love to believe it. You're still affiliated with the GRU, aren't you?"

"No."

He lied, and we both knew it. The two Russian secret police forces were always at each other's throats over jurisdiction, especially in foreign operations. The defection of a high ranking GRU officer meant valuable infighting points at the Kremlin.

"Let's discuss the matter outside." I pushed him through the tent flap and toward the tank getting its tread fixed. The instant I saw the tank, everything fell into place for me.

"Shoot me and be done with it, Carter. You Americans are such sentimental fools. Or is this revenge?"

"The other tank's tread is broken, also," I barked at the technicians. "Fix it first. Leave this one."

Suslovitch started to speak. I rammed my Luger directly into his spine to keep him silent. Seeing their commander with me, the technicians obeyed, mumbling under their breaths about idiot officers and Russian bureaucracy.

"Into our limousine," I ordered. Suslovitch climbed up. I slugged him just as he attempted to swing the turret machine gun around. The colonel sagged into the tight cockpit. I crammed him down further, then dropped on top of him. He didn't stir. Strapping him into the assistant driver's seat, I began warming the diesels. In the cold, they were slow to turn over but perseverance finally won. Roaring, belching noxious black smoke, the engines ran at full RPM.

I slammed the tank into gear and caromed into the

night. The tread the technicians had been working on came loose and started pulling the tank to the right. For a ghastly moment, I thought all the tank would do was turn in circles. Continual jerking back and forth on the steering levers gave me a spastic course, but one aimed out of the camp.

Somewhere along the way, the guards decided the tank wasn't supposed to be leaving. I heard the sharp *pings*! as light machine gun fire bounced off the thick steel hull. Past the last of the sentries and over the plain I drove the tank, swerving to and fro like a skier down a mountain.

Safety.

Or was it? I worried over the feeling I had in my gut. I'd missed something. I'd chosen this tank because the other's cannon had been jammed. The last thing in the world I wanted was to be a sitting duck out in the middle of the plain for the other one's gun. Stopping to check, I pushed up the crude periscope and peered behind.

The other tank's cannon was still jammed, but there wasn't anything wrong with its locomotion system. Its crew had been on the ball. They'd started up immediately and charged after me. I had a gun, they had maneuverability and speed. And they were less than a hundred yards behind. Playing bumper-cars with tanks isn't recommended, especially when my tank lacked mobility.

Suslovitch still slumped in his seat. I took the chance of parking, heaving one of the large 105mm rounds into the breach, locking and cocking, then sitting back down in the driver's seat. The turret mechanism worked pretty well. Electric humming filled the interior of the tank as I spun around, sighted and fired.

I missed the approaching tank, but my shell hit enough in front so that they swerved in reaction. This gave me time to load another shell, get into the driver's seat again and press the firing button. Now I had them square in the sights.

But nothing happened. Again I stabbed down on the firing button. Nothing. Jammed.

"Damn," I said with feeling, beginning to work the

steering levers and gun the tank for the far side of the valley. If I reached terrain controlled by the Old Man of the Mountains, I had a chance. Otherwise, the other tank would ram me.

That's exactly what they did. Their superior speed and handling let them overtake me in less than a minute. They must have realized my cannon had jammed; they smashed hard into the back of my tank, hard enough to slam me forward. I chipped a tooth on the control panel and the whiplash sent a jolt of pain all the way down my spine.

Turn, swerve, stop, I did it all trying to evade. One in three tries was successful. The other two times got me bone-jarring impacts. My hands sweated and I felt like a milk shake inside. The one time I tried to turn the tables and ram the other Soviet tank almost upended me. My good tread dug in and spun me in a circle, over the edge of a ravine. Gunning the motors at the right instant kept me level.

They hit me again.

Smoke began filling the cockpit. Electrical insulation burned. The controls got harder and harder to handle. This old bus was nearing the end of its run.

But one humming noise caught my attention. The fire control lights had all turned green again. Whatever had jammed the cannon before had been knocked back into the proper firing order.

I didn't waste a second. The turret swung around. The silhouette of the other tank loomed on the bank of the ravine. At less than twenty yards, I fired. The roar of the cannon deafened me; the secondary roar as the other tank exploded echoed even louder.

Tiny flames lapped under the control panel now. Time to bail out. Pulling Suslovitch with me, I opened the turret hatch and was treated to a shower of droplets of molten steel. My shot had been too good for a casual walk under the stars. Clothes smouldering, skin blistered from the remains of the other tank dropping from the skies, I dragged Arkady Suslovitch behind me.

None too soon. Flames exploded inside my tank,

belching up and out the open turret hatch. If I hadn't gotten out when I did, that tank would have been my personal crematorium.

I continued dragging Suslovitch with me. Slowly, my hearing returned. The first thing I heard was music to my ears: bolts on rifles slamming home.

The Old Man of the Mountains' men had found me.

TWENTY-EIGHT

"The KGB man that was talking with Suslovitch is the one in charge," I said, putting down my binoculars.

The way the troops had formed, then deployed to await still another full frontal charge from Kali's faithful warriors showed that someone with a little sense of tactics was in command. I glanced over to where Arkady Suslovitch lay bound and gagged. The Russian colonel hadn't been any worse for the wear and tear I'd put on him the night before. He'd even survived the tank battering better than I had. Now he was forced to sit and watch his men go down to defeat.

I hoped that the KGB officer who'd been talking to Suslovitch last night didn't have his fine touch for tactics.

"You can't make another frontal assault," I told the Old Man. "You saw what happened yesterday."

"Yes," he said solemnly, "they retreated. If we attack again in that manner, they will retreat even more."

"Their two tanks are out of action, but more are on the way. They're due to arrive any time now."

"Within the hour," confirmed the Old Man. His sources of information never ceased to amaze me. He really knew all that happened, no matter where in the Hindu Kush it occurred.

"Then don't waste the lives of your followers."

He thought about this for a while before answering. When he did, a slight tremor had come into his voice. I felt the strain asking imposed on him.

"What do you suggest?"

"They're backed into the mouth of the Khyber Pass. Attack along the walls of the mountains. One group from the left, another from the right. Keep your main body of men directly in front, but don't attack. If the Russians come out, then use them. Otherwise, hammer at their flanks, try to seal them into the pass. Without the tank, they can't break out. If they do, let some of them come, then redouble the attack from the flank and cut them off. As long as the mountains protect you—"

"Kali protects us," he cut in.

"As long as the mountains and Kali protect you, the Soviets aren't going anywhere. They'll be stoppered up." From the way Suslovitch squirmed, I knew the plan was a good one.

Again, the Old Man's silent communications network went into action. I don't know what he did, but down on the plains facing the pass, the main body of men broke into three sections. Two went to flank the Russians, while the majority stayed in place. Almost instant transmission of his orders and yet he hadn't moved. I didn't pretend to understand how it was done. Maybe the goddess Kali herself came and gave the orders to the faithful.

I paced, waiting for the battle to really begin. The KGB man in charge didn't dare sit too long in the Khyber Pass. He had to make the effort to break through, to get on into the Pakistani heartland. Suslovitch had failed to consolidate and make a strong base here. His successor might decide to leave behind these savage mountain cultists and try to establish a base in friendlier terrain.

"Nick, Gupta is weakening," said Ananda.

I took her in my arms. This was all I could do to comfort her. Her brother's life hung by a slender thread that none of us dared touch.

"I won't lie and tell you it'll be all right," I said. "He's probably going to die. If . . . if the battle's over quickly enough, then we can try to get help for him. Until then. . ."

"I understand. When he is coherent, he boasts of his bravery in Afghanistan."

"Rightfully so."

"He said you promised him a medal. From your President."

"I told him the United States never forgets her friends. The medal is something that higher-ups have to decide on. But I assure you, I'll do what I can to get one for him. No matter what."

"Thank you." Ananda turned and started away.

The echoes of gunfire disturbed the stillness. Picking up my binoculars, I scanned the battlegrounds. The Old Man had placed his men well. The Russians were trapped. As the firing continued, I saw Russian units breaking and retreating. This time it wasn't an orderly withdrawal. They panicked and ran. I didn't blame them. After knowing what Kali promised from the ordeal the day before, their nerves had to be shot waiting for that screaming, knife-wielding horde to again flow over their line. Without the tanks for heavy support, the foot soldiers stood little chance.

As I watched, I carefully plotted what to do with Suslovitch. Looking at the man convinced me he would never willingly turn traitor and denounce the U.S.S.R. In his way, he was as much a patriot as I was. But a better way of using him came to me. Contented with my idea, I turned back to study the ebb and flow of the battle.

It went well for the cultists. Very well.

Until the Soviet tanks roared out of the pass. Three of them broke out, belching fumes, their turrets looking this way and that like giant questing metallic beetles.

"Get your men back," I told the Old Man. "Those tanks will destroy them."

"We fight. Now!"

Even as he shouted the word, the entire plain came alive. I can't begin to estimate how many men rushed forward. Ten thousand? A hundred thousand? It might have been the full half million he had bragged about. However many it was, the sheer numbers made the casualty rate even worse. They got in each other's way and allowed the machine guns and cannon on the tanks to knock them down and blow them up as if they were little more than targets in a shotting gallery.

The Russian foot soldiers stayed well back in the Khyber Pass and let the tanks do the real dirty work. Tired, I sat down on a rock, head in hands. The thugs would continue to batter themselves, their knives, their fists against the armored might of those tanks until every last man had died a bloody death. Still, in a way, I'd done my job. The Russians had been slowed down. Hawk hadn't really expected me to actually stop a major Russian invasion.

But I'd expected it of myself.

The roar of jets brought my gaze up. A flight of MIG-23s with Indian markings wheeled overhead, then dived. The air filled with smoky contrails as the air-to-ground missiles blasted craters around the tanks.

"Pull your men back," I shouted to the Old Man. "Let the jets take out the tanks."

Kali's worshipers dissolved into the landscape, leaving the titans to blast at one another. Pass after pass from the jets inflicted mounting damage on the three tanks. One direct hit blew the turret off the lead tank. The gouts of flame spewing from the interior told the story.

The other two tanks whined as they engaged gears and headed back for the Khyber Pass. The Indian Air Force MIGs, so gratefully furnished by the generous Soviet Union to their valued ally, blasted apart tanks built by the same factory.

The MIGs wing-wobbled to signal anyone on the ground that they had to depart, then reformed their V-shaped squadron. In less than a minute, they vanished down the valley, out of sight in the towering peaks on either side.

The slaughter this time was as one-sided as before— but the sides had changed. Stark fanaticism spooked the Russian troops. They were routed by Kali's screaming assassins.

Only a single living Russian remained on this side of

the border. I smiled at Arkady Suslovitch, who now lay still and defeated. He had seen the brief battle and knew that the Soviet Union might never win its warm water port now, at least in Pakistan.

"It's over," I said to the Old Man of the Mountains. "Kali has triumphed." Without another word, he turned and walked off, head held high. He and his men returned to their mountain fortress, perhaps for another hundred years until they were again needed to defend Pakistani sovereignty. I was glad to see him go.

"What happens now, Nick?" asked Ananda.

"I've got to leave. My mission is accomplished, more than accomplished. I was supposed to report back and do what I could to slow down Suslovitch's troops. They ended up exposing themselves as Russian units and left enough hardware to indict them in any world court. World opinion will be against them."

"And him?" Ananda pointed to Suslovitch.

"That's icing on the cake. Living proof that it wasn't just the Mujeheddin from Afghanistan trying to stir up trouble by using stolen Russian equipment." I moved closer to her and held her in my arms. "Colonel Suslovitch's going to do even more. I might not be able to get your brother that medal from the President of the United States, but Gupta might get one from Pakistan."

"Our country? Why? Because of what he did in Afghanistan?"

"He shouldn't mention that. Not ever. It brings up a way for the Russians to make countercharges. If a Pakistani force attacked a Soviet air base in Afghanistan, they can claim this was only a retaliatory raid. No, here's what you tell the authorities. Gupta Dasai singlehandedly captured the Russian commander. Nothing else."

"But you, Nick, what about you?"

"Me?" I said, smiling wryly. "I never existed."

DON'T MISS THE NEXT NEW NICK CARTER SPY THRILLER

OPERATION VENDETTA

I'd already decided that I'd used up the major portion of my luck getting to the Cherlovitch farm without being detected. Going back, I was convinced I'd run into a patrol. If I did, I wanted to have the advantage of speed. The speedometer on the motorcycle, an old American model, was set for a hundred and twenty. I'd settle for half that.

"Don't forget, Nadia," I said as the girl settled into the sidecar on top of the weapons and covered herself with another blanket. "If we're stopped, I can't hear or speak. And you're in great pain from your appendicitis attack."

"Yes," she said. "Understanding perfectly well."

I rammed the cycle and sidecar around the barn and house, then stopped beside the road. Nadia looked at me, puzzled.

"One little job left to do," I said.

I took my Luger from its holster and walked back through the weed-choked yard. If Mark Koselke ever decided to start up his vendetta again, at least he wouldn't be able to use the weapons he'd stashed in the shed.

I fired through the open door, into a crate of bazooka shells. Even before the great blast of fire and air blew the shed to bits, I was halfway back to the motorcycle. I leaped on, opened up the throttle and looked back only once.

The shed was gone, but shells and grenades and cartridges were still thudding and popping. By the time the local police or the nearest army contingent reached this noisy place, I hoped to be far, far away.

When we reached sixty miles per hour, I eased back and listened to the engine rumble and roar. The cool dawn wind felt good on my face. My feet liked the metal supports much better than they'd liked the road and the fields. Everything was humming along well.

Until we came within five miles of Rostov.

At a major intersection, two soldiers sat in a Russian version of a jeep. I could see them from a great distance, just sitting there as though they were sound asleep. But they'd been watching us as long as I'd been watching them.

I didn't even slow. I kept the cycle at a steady sixty and waved to the soldiers as we whizzed through the intersection. Through the rear-view mirror, I saw the headlights on the jeep snap to life, saw the jeep surge into the intersection and start after us. I kept going, as though I hadn't seen.

When the siren wailed, I continued on; after all, I was supposed to be deaf.

Nadia played her role well. She reached up and tugged my sleeve and pointed toward the following jeep. I hoped the soldiers were close enough to take notice. I turned, smiled at the soldiers and began to slow. I stopped on the berm and waited, smiling at the soldiers, waiting to twitch my forearm muscles and to put Hugo into action if necessary.

The soldiers sauntered up and said something in a Russian accent that I didn't recognize. Nadia responded, saying I was deaf and didn't hear the siren. The conversation went on and on. I lost the gist of it, but Nadia remained calm. Once, though, when I glanced down at her, there was the look of real pain on her face. When one of the soldiers said something about our papers, Nadia groaned and let out a little yip of pain. The soldiers nodded. One of them patted my shoulder and muttered something in Russian. I smiled, even though I knew the soldier had called me a filthy name just to test me.

Finally, Nadia motioned to me that it was all right to go. I saluted the soldiers, throwing a little idiocy into my deaf-mute act, and turned the throttle. The jeep sat beside the road for a long time, then I saw that it was turning around, heading back to the intersection.

"Good job, Nadia," I said. "But what would you have done if they'd insisted on seeing our papers?"

"Would have shot them," Nadia said calmly.

Shocked, I glanced down at her. She was holding one of Mark Koselke's .30 caliber rifles. She had the bolt in place and a cartridge in the chamber.

Yep, I thought, this kid is a survivor. We might make it.

Might.

We still had a long way to go.

The next intersection was on top of a rise in the ground. As we approached it, I surveyed the perpendicular road in each direction, saw nothing. But, as I was making a turn to the left, to circle the city, I saw the personnel carrier about two miles to the west.

Soldiers were milling around it, waiting.

Waiting, no doubt, for us.

—From OPERATION VENDETTA
A New Nick Carter Spy Thriller
From Charter in June

☐ 01948-X	**THE AMAZON**	$2.50
☐ 05381-5	**BEIRUT INCIDENT**	$2.25
☐ 10505-X	**THE CHRISTMAS KILL**	$2.50
☐ 13935-3	**DAY OF THE DINGO**	$1.95
☐ 14172-2	**THE DEATH STAR AFFAIR**	$2.50
☐ 14169-2	**DEATHLIGHT**	$2.50
☐ 15676-2	**DOCTOR DNA**	$2.50
☐ 15244-9	**THE DOMINICAN AFFAIR**	$2.50
☐ 17014-5	**THE DUBROVNIK MASSACRE**	$2.25
☐ 18124-4	**EARTH SHAKER**	$2.50

☐ 33068-1	**HIDE AND GO DIE**	$2.50
☐ 29782-X	**THE GOLDEN BULL**	$2.25
☐ 30272-6	**THE GREEK SUMMIT**	$2.50
☐ 34909-9	**THE HUMAN TIME BOMB**	$2.25
☐ 34999-4	**THE HUNTER**	$2.50
☐ 35868-3	**THE INCA DEATH SQUAD**	$2.50
☐ 35881-0	**THE ISRAELI CONNECTION**	$2.50
☐ 47183-8	**THE LAST SAMURAI**	$2.50
☐ 58866-2	**NORWEGIAN TYPHOON**	$2.50
☐ 64433-3	**THE OUTBACK GHOSTS**	$2.50

Available at your local bookstore or return this form to:

 CHARTER BOOKS
Book Mailing Service
P.O. Box 690, Rockville Centre, NY 11571

Please send me the titles checked above. I enclose _____.
Include $1.00 for postage and handling if one book is ordered; 50¢ per book for
two or more. California, Illinois, New York and Tennessee residents please add
sales tax. (allow six weeks for delivery)

NAME _____

ADDRESS _____

CITY _____ STATE/ZIP _____

A8